fill

in

the

blank

Look for more books in

The Friendship Ring Series:

if you only knew (Zoe's story)

please, please, please (CJ's story)

not that i care (Morgan's story)

what are friends for? (Olivia's story)

popularity contest (Zoe's story)

Rachel Vail's

The Friendship Ring Series

fill
in
the
blank

AN APPLE PAPERBACK / SCHOLASTIC INC.

New York • Toronto • London • Auckland • Sydney
Mexico City • New Delhi • Hong Kong

ISBN 0-590-68914-2

12 11 10 9 8 7 6 5 4 3 2 1   0 1 2 3 4 5/0

Printed in the U.S.A.   40
First Scholastic printing, May 2000

For Liam,

who scrunches his face with delight,

and teaches me fresh about love

one

"You're the man," I told my reflection.

"You're gonna miss the bus!" Mom yelled up.

I checked my watch. Mom was right. I gave up on the hair, which looked fine, really, pretty good, and charged downstairs, grabbing my backpack off the landing and my lunch out of Mom's hand.

"You're welcome!" she called to my back.

Over the fence, through the Grandons' yard, a flat-out sprint all the way to the bus stop, where the bus wasn't, yet. Just Zoe Grandon, my back-door neighbor, and my twin brother, Jonas. Zoe was staring up the street to where the bus should've been coming from. Jonas was staring at Zoe. I looked from Jonas to her and back again.

"What?" I asked them both.

Jonas pointed his thumb at her. "Something's wrong with Zoe."

"What's wrong with her?" I asked him, smoothing down my hair. It was a very cool haircut, way better than Jonas's, with his floppy curls in front and prickly shaved part up the back.

"How should I know what's wrong with her?" Jonas asked me. He wears his backpack over both shoulders and mostly keeps his hands in his pockets, but he had a point.

"OK," I said, and tapped Zoe on the head. "Hey. What's wrong with you?"

"Shut up," she said. "There's nothing wrong with me."

"She says there's nothing wrong with her," I told Jonas.

"I don't know," Jonas said. "I guess she's just really interested in where the bus is."

"You guys!" She was trying not to laugh.

We both said, "What?"

Zoe dropped her books. She shoved me with one hand and Jonas with the other. I only stumbled back one step before I dropped my books, too, and charged back at her. She's not like a girl who you have to be all careful around: She can fight better than Jonas, not that he's much of a bruiser, and she likes to fight, more than he does, too. She's like me — you know, sarcastic, a wise guy.

So I was about to shove her back when she stepped away and held up her hand. She stood up out of her fighting stance and said, in this weird snotty voice, "It just would've been nice if you guys had offered us a ride to Olivia's yesterday."

I dropped my fists, too, and was, like, *What?* Then I crouched back down, figuring it was a trick and she was about to knock the wind out of me. I smiled, but Zoe didn't.

She took another step backward and snarled, "Seriously."

"When?"

"After the pizza. You know," she said. "After we got school supplies and everything. When your mom came."

Jonas and I looked at each other, like, *Is she nuts? Or joking?*

Probably joking, I realized. She, Morgan Miller, and CJ Hurley were walking to this geeky kid Olivia's house. Me and Jonas couldn't go because we had to get these haircuts, so our mother picked us up. Zoe was probably leading up to something, some complicated joke, maybe. There's always something going on with Zoe. She's always setting you up for a put-down. You have to watch out.

I looked at her sideways, trying to get her to crack a smile, which she was trying her hardest not to, I could tell. She's really devious, but I've known her forever, so she can't fool me. She looked away, scared she was going to lose it.

"If you wanted a ride, you should've just asked," Jonas told her as the bus squealed down the hill toward us. "We were just going to the barber. Our mother wouldn't care."

"Yeah, but," Zoe argued, and shook her head without continuing. It was weird to see her not being able to shoot down Jonas. There wasn't much she could say, really. She knows our mother would rather give her a ride than us. I squinted at her. Zoe Grandon doesn't end up speechless against Jonas. No way, never. She was obviously setting up something I couldn't figure out. I realized I was grinning in anticipation.

"And Tommy teased CJ about her bun," she said.

"Huh?" I asked. "CJ?" She went up the bus steps behind Jonas while I tried to figure out what in the world she was talking about. I poked her on the shoulder. "Hurley?"

"You know another CJ?" she muttered.

"I didn't tease her," I said, poking Zoe harder. She didn't turn around, just kept going up the aisle toward the back.

I've never teased CJ Hurley in my life, about anything. She's not the teasing type. Her bun? What the — oh, her hair? I hadn't teased CJ about her hair; I just asked her why she always wears it up. She said it was for ballet, so I pointed out that she wasn't dancing ballet then as we all walked to Sundries to buy school supplies. Excuse me for being interested! CJ is the only celebrity in our grade, dancing every year in *The Nutcracker,* and I've always wanted to ask her about it. I wasn't teasing her. She's not like Zoe. If you teased CJ, she might cry or something.

"I didn't tease her about it," I told Zoe. "I asked her about it."

I sat down next to big, dorky Lou Hochstetter, who asked, "Who?"

"Nobody," I mumbled.

Zoe sat down next to Jonas and nodded at me. "Nice haircut."

"Yeah?" I asked, and looked quickly for a comeback. "Nice knee," I said, nodding at her scabbed-up leg.

"Uh-oh," murmured Lou, who knows better than to get into it with Zoe. He flattened his face to the seat like I could shield him or something.

But Zoe didn't say anything back. I waited the whole bus ride. Nothing.

Jonas and I shrugged at each other on the way in to

school. I decided to forget about it. Over Labor Day weekend, I had this idea: I was going to buckle down and concentrate on my schoolwork, apply myself, as Mr. Toole suggested I should in the conference my parents were hauled in for last year. So yesterday, since it was the first day of seventh grade, I was amazingly focused. Today I'm over it. Phew. Lasted shorter than a cold, and about as annoying. I spaced out all through the morning.

At lunch, Jonas and I ate ours and were still hungry, so we wandered over to the girls' table to see what we could grub. I was just climbing into the bench when CJ Hurley whispered to Zoe, "You must be so upset."

"Why?" I asked. "What happened?"

"Nothing," Morgan Miller said in that same snotty voice Zoe had used this morning.

"OK," I said, scouting around for what desserts they had. Jonas nabbed some pretzel sticks from Olivia Pogostin.

As he was chomping down, Morgan Miller snorted, "You could ask!"

Jonas put the half-eaten sticks back into the box and said, "Sorry."

We got up. Obviously there was no chowing opportunity.

"Later," I said.

"Much," Zoe answered.

The thing is, that is just not a Zoe comeback. Way too obvious, way too, well, Morgan-ish. The girls were all giggling as we left.

"What's up with them?" I asked Jonas.

He shrugged.

"Zoe's been acting weird to me all day, don't you think?"

Jonas turned and stared at me.

"What?" I asked.

He slowly smiled.

I shoved him. "Shut up."

"Mom's right, maybe," he said.

"Maybe NOT." I grabbed a handful of mini marshmallows from Lou and chucked them at the girls, to prove to Jonas he was wrong, just like Mom is. I do NOT have a crush on Zoe. Not in the least. Nothing could be further from the truth.

two

Jonas and I stood at the kitchen counter, staring at our reflections in the window while we ate fried chicken and listened to the garage door groaning shut behind our parents' car.

"Beautiful," Jonas said.

He's not usually the sarcastic one. I raised my eyebrows at him. "Yeah, and yours is lovely, too."

"My what?" Jonas asked.

"What are you staring at?" I asked him, grabbing another drumstick.

"The moon," he said.

Oh. I looked through my reflection. There was a full moon. So apparently I was the only one staring at myself.

"Pretty amazing-looking tonight, isn't it?" Jonas asked. "The moonlight?"

I punched him in the arm. "Shut up."

"No, I mean it," he swore. "I wasn't . . ."

"Yeah, right," I said with my mouth full. "Hey. What do you think Zoe meant when she said 'nice haircut' this morning?"

"Maybe she thinks you got a nice haircut," he said, shrugging. "Just a guess."

"Yeah, right."

"You *do*!"

"Thank you," I said, touching my hair and willing my cheeks not to get red. I knew what he meant, of course.

"Not 'have a nice haircut.'" He hiked himself up onto the counter and sat there, smirking at me.

"Well, you should see yours, Q-Tip head," I said. I dumped the chicken bones in the garbage and went into the den to watch TV.

I settled in for a nice long night of zoning out. It was Mom and Dad's anniversary, and they'd gone out to dinner all the way to Springfield, so they'd be gone a good long time. I pulled the fleece blanket over my legs and stretched out along the length of the couch. If Jonas wanted to watch, he could take the chair. What you get for being slow. And thinking you know everything going on in some other person's mind. Which he doesn't.

As if I'd be interested in doing anything with Zoe but beating her butt in tennis. I flipped through some channels, looking for anything the slightest bit interesting. Jonas is so stupid, with that smirk.

I heard him going up the stairs. Jonas sits in his chair at his desk to read. Even *Sports Illustrated,* he won't lie on the couch. He says he concentrates better. Whatever. When we went with the girls yesterday to buy school supplies, he took forever, everybody waiting for him, all the girls standing there trying to be patient in the heat, shading their eyes out on the sidewalk while Jonas made sure he got the exact kind of compass we were supposed to, with the blunt tip or the pointy, whichever it was Ms. Cress recommended, as if that would make all the difference in his life. And this is my twin. Obviously not identical.

"Mom said not to watch the whole Thursday-night lineup," Jonas yelled down to me.

"Mom says a lot of things," I answered. *"How do you feel about starting seventh grade?"* I imitated.

I heard Jonas laughing. The day before school she must've asked us once an hour how we were feeling about starting seventh grade. *Come on, boys, talk to me.* Jonas told her he was both nervous and excited. I burped every time she asked, until it finally became clear she wasn't going to let up, so I said, *I don't know*. I say I don't know to my mother about twenty times a day.

I turned up the volume to drown out the annoying Jonas-like worries in my stupid head, like, *Why is Zoe mad at me?* I told myself I was just reading way too much into things. *Nervous and excited*. Give me a break. The great thing about Zoe is that she's totally normal, like one of the guys. You can say "nice knee" to her, and she doesn't freak out and whisper what a jerk you are to all her friends. If I suddenly had to worry about Zoe's feelings along with everybody else's, I think I'd have to shoot myself.

But still, even with the TV blasting, I couldn't help thinking that Zoe was acting weird, and what bugged me was I couldn't figure out why. What Jonas was saying at lunch is just a load of crap. He reads so much into everything. Just because I noticed that Zoe was acting weird to me? I notice things; I'm observant. That's all. I noticed CJ wears her hair up. Does that mean I have a crush on her, too? A lot of people are observant. Reporters, cops, spies. It doesn't mean they want to go out with somebody, it's just staying sharp, like the best basketball players can see the whole court without moving their eyes. It's the same thing. Jonas with his smirking, like he *knows,* when he knows noth-ing. He stinks at basketball, and this is probably ex-actly why.

"You stink at basketball," I yelled up to him. He didn't answer, which pissed me off that much more. I turned up the volume enough to blast him upstairs. It's only the first week of school; how much home-work does he think he has? Some people don't know how to pace themselves.

I cranked the volume even louder and yelled, "It's starting!" although we both knew it was still too early.

three

I woke up hearing Jonas calling for Mom.

I listened for her footsteps to come running down the hall toward our rooms, but didn't hear them.

"Mom?" Jonas asked again. His voice was shaking.

Nothing.

"Mom?"

I pushed my blanket away and padded across my carpet to my door. Leaning against the corner of the hallway where my door and Jonas's come to an angle, I asked him, "Windmill Man?"

"Yeah," he answered weakly.

I rubbed my eyes. His room was dark except for the little night-light he still needs on his night table, which lit up the gray-and-white pinstripes of his sheets and comforter. I could see his body, in the horizontal stripes of his blue-and-green pajamas, lying uncovered on his bed. His eyes were closed, and his chest was moving up and down quickly.

"I'll get her," I said.

As I walked down the hallway to my parents' room, I could hear water running in the shower, which meant they must've gotten home not long ago, pretty late. Jonas had come down after he finished all his homework, the grind, and fallen asleep on the other end of the couch from me before the news. When I caught myself dozing off during the financial report (Dow closing down three points), I woke him, and we trudged up to bed without brushing our teeth, since Mom and Dad still weren't here to make us.

They'd gone out to celebrate their twentieth wedding anniversary. It's a pretty big deal; there's going to be a huge party this weekend for them. Jonas and I had to get blue sport jackets, and also, of course, the haircuts.

I ran my fingers through my short hair as I walked down the hallway toward my parents' room, hearing the insistent pulsing of the shower water. My hair felt bristly, rough under my hand, unfamiliar. It had grown a lot over the summer, and I'd gotten used to it. *Nice haircut.* Hmm, I'd been awake more than a minute before I thought of that again; getting better.

I expected my father to be propped in bed on his mounds of pillows, with his glasses on, reading one of the fat books of nonfiction he's always sneaking off to devour. Drives Mom crazy. But if she's in the shower or talking to us, or something, he can sneak away and learn about Lyndon Johnson or a controversial scientific scandal from the 1880s, sometimes standing in the hall to save the time of bending his knees and sitting down, an extra paragraph before he's caught.

But he wasn't in the bed, wasn't standing with his tie loosened in front of his closet. "Dad?" I asked softly.

The door to the bathroom was slightly open. Strands of steam curled out. If he was down in the kitchen having a glass of Kahlua while she showered, it meant they'd had an argument.

"Dad?"

No answer.

When they fight, she talks fast and clipped and says things like, "I need you to listen to me for five continuous minutes without opening a book, closing your eyes, or moaning." And he says, "I'm sorry," and she says, "I'm not done criticizing you yet, so you can hold off on that apology until you hear me out." Sometimes he laughs, and her face softens, her voice slows down a little, and Jonas and I can relax, but other times, she gets in the shower before the softening, and then Dad has a Kahlua and finds something to criticize me about, within twelve hours at most. My family is totally predictable. The second and the fourth step going from the main level of our house up to the bedrooms both squeak. If you need to sneak upstairs, you have to skip those two stairs, hit only one, three, and the top landing. You just have to know how to do it. Likewise with the people; the key is knowing what to avoid. So I made my way around their neatly made bed and tried not to bang into the vertical blinds on the window as I passed them, tiptoeing toward the steamy bathroom. Banging the blinds is a noise that drives my father crazy. He can hear it from the basement.

I leaned on the doorknob of the bathroom and swung the top half of myself into the steamy bathroom and said, "Mom?"

She gasped. She backed up; I could make out her movements through the mottled light reflected off the hammered-looking glass of the shower door, through the thick fog of their all-white bathroom.

"Tommy?" But it was my father's voice from inside the shower, asking my name. He sounded serious, like he was calling on one of the teenagers in his history class at the high school to come up to the board and argue a position. "Is that Tommy or Jonas?"

I didn't answer. I turned around to leave the woozy heat of their bathroom and closed their bathroom door on my way out. *OK*, I thought, *whatever that was going on in there, I don't want to know.*

At the linen closet, I extracted a white towel (one of theirs; ours are yellow to match our bathroom) from the jumbled heaps of sheets and towels crammed in the linen closet, which doesn't close completely unless you really coordinate it, pushing with your foot and your hip at the same time as you turn the doorknob and let it catch. I swung it toward closed, but left it gaping open. Mom hates that, says it makes the whole house look unkempt.

I went to mine and Jonas's bathroom, filled a Dixie cup with warmish water, and went into Jonas's room. He's been having this same nightmare for a long time and, since my room is right next door to his, I've seen Mom handle it enough times to know what you have to do. I wasn't about to do all the cooing and sighing like she does; just drop off the stuff and get back to bed. She babies him too much.

I turned on his light. He blinked his eyes and sat up. "Where's Mom?"

"Don't ask," I told myself as much as him, thinking, *You don't want to know.* I plunked the cup of water on his night table and avoided eye contact. "Sit up."

He did and sipped the water while I lay the towel down on the damp sweaty area of his bed. "He almost caught me that time," Jonas said between sips. "I heard the thrashing arms, right behind me. I felt one of them scrape my shoulder."

"I told you what you should do," I reminded him.

"I can't, Tommy."

"If you did, he'd lose all his power. I swear." I flipped his pillow over so the dry side was up. "You just have to turn around and face him."

Jonas crumpled the paper cup, put it on his night table, and lay back down.

"You need new pajamas?"

"I'm OK," he said, and closed his eyes.

"OK," I said. I know Mom usually sits on his bed after a nightmare and reassures him for a while, but I didn't think I was up for that. I kind of patted him on the head twice, but that wasn't great, either, so I stepped back. The water and the pillow flip would have to be good enough.

I heard the water in Mom and Dad's bathroom shut off.

"So," I said, but couldn't think of anything else. I

can't hear what Mom says to him, just the murmur of her voice. I pulled his blankets up over him, let them fall loosely around him. I wasn't about to start pushing and tucking, fussing over him. He's old enough to adjust his own blankets.

He whispered, "Thanks," and then, when I was halfway across his room, "Sorry."

"Don't worry." I turned off his light and said, "'Night" on my way out. Then I sprinted to my bed and slid in fast, pulling my pillow over my head.

four

before my alarm, my eyes opened and I was wide-awake. 6:32. Friday. In my room. I've been doing this lately, waking up joltingly, then lying in my bed taking stock, making sure I have a handle on who I am and where, and when, as if somehow while I'm sleeping and not in control, everything might have been switched on me or taken away.

Third day of seventh grade. *How do you feel about that? Nervous? Excited?*

I heard Jonas's alarm go off. He just lets it buzz for a while, then hits the snooze. You'd think such a perfectionist would pop out of bed the first time around, but no. He goes for two, sometimes three snoozes.

I decided to get ready fast, beat everybody down to

the kitchen, and maybe even be early to the bus stop for a change, not have to chase it down the street and collapse into a seat sweaty and panting, with Zoe staring at me calmly with that little grin on her face, saying things.

In the bathroom, I rested my hands on the counter and leaned toward the mirror. *Nice haircut.*

Shut up!

I inspected my face in the mirror, searching for any new hairs on my upper lip. Nothing. Jonas had a few, I had noticed, near the corners of his mouth, a few little, dark stragglers. He hasn't said anything, but I'm sure he's keeping track. An old razor of my father's and a can of shaving cream had materialized in the medicine cabinet over the summer. I don't know if Jonas has seen it, or who put it there. Dad's way of subtle male-bonding? Mom's little joke on her smooth-cheeked sons?

Gideon Weld shaved already; he constantly rubs his stubbly chin like it's a magic lamp and a genie might pop out of his mouth any second. But I think he's the only seventh-grade boy who has. We're not behind or anything, me and Jonas. Those little stragglers he's so proud of are not nearly enough to shave. Not too many of the eighth-grade boys shave, even, I don't think.

I brushed my teeth, watching myself in the mirror. After I spit, I turned around and moved the curtain aside to look out the bathroom window. Zoe's shade was open. I ducked and kept watching, but nobody seemed to be moving in there. Maybe they were already downstairs for breakfast. Her dad makes a very big deal of breakfast, of food in general. I love going over there for breakfast — french toast, eggs, omelets any way you want. My stomach grumbled, imagining it.

She asked me the other night, when we were hitting tennis balls against my garage, who my best friend is, and I said Jonas, of course. It's automatic. I never really thought about it before she asked. But in some ways, even though he's my twin and I would do anything for him, protect him and look out for him, all that, I actually have more in common with Zoe. Maybe because there's less at stake. Nobody has told me I have to wait up for her or watch out for her or think how she's feeling; nobody said it's a tie when we race and I win, the way it is and always has been with Jonas. With Zoe, it's just relaxed, no problems. She didn't mention who her best friend is. A lot of people probably would list Zoe as their best friend. That's just how she is; everybody likes her. Who wouldn't want her as a best friend? You know she'll always be honestly happy for you if something good happens and, like, if she had one piece of gum, she'd want to split it with the whole class.

As I was standing there in the bathroom thinking about her, she walked into her room. I sat down quickly on the floor, my heart pounding. What if she glanced out her window and caught me? Knowing her, she'd probably just smile and wave, or throw open her window and challenge me to a race to the bus stop. I swallowed hard and then slapped myself across the face.

I turned on the shower without risking another peek out the window. As I stepped out of my boxers, I reached into the medicine cabinet and grabbed the razor and shaving cream to take in with me. I locked the door. The bathroom doors in our house actually do have locks.

I lathered up my hair while I read the shaving cream can: "Leave skin wet. Put gel on fingertips. Gently rub over skin to lather and shave."

Thanks guys, very helpful. They cover the obvious parts — that you're supposed to apply the stuff to your skin (As opposed to? Your teeth?) — but leave out things like which direction to go with the razor, what your grip is supposed to be, how hard to drag it. Things that might actually help a person.

I plucked off the cap and pushed the top button. A

quick jism of gel squirted into my other hand. Blue, cool, gooey. Tilting my head back into the spray to rinse out some of the dripping shampoo, I stared at the glob of blue on my fingers. Then I rubbed my hands together, and the clear blue was transformed into thick white lather.

I got an eyeful of water and shampoo. Cursing, I turned to face the spray and wiped my eye with the back of my wrist, and got stung with a dab of the shaving cream, which had my eye tearing like crazy. Divine punishment for cursing, obviously. A couple of deep breaths later, I regained my vision and rubbed the remaining shaving cream off my fingers onto my arm.

Then I took some more and lathered up my whole forearm.

I picked up the razor and wondered if I was nuts. The blade was sharp, I saw quickly as I sliced into the tip of my left index finger, testing it. It didn't hurt; I only knew it had cut me by the two dots of red.

OK, then. I mowed a line of shaving cream off my arm, up to my elbow, with the razor. The skin revealed was tan and smooth. After I rinsed the razor, I mowed another straight streak.

A knock on the door.

My "I'm in here!" sounded a little more frantic than I'd intended.

"Taking a vacation?" was all I heard of Jonas's reply, and some rattling of the doorknob.

I didn't answer, just tried to concentrate and speed up. He was knocking again, and I heard him calling Mom, so I finished my left arm and rinsed it. My left hand is sort of shaky and uncoordinated. If I tried using the razor with it, I might need stitches all up my right arm, and then have to explain to everyone why in the world I had been shaving my arms. Not that I could explain. Not that I would, even if I could. I'd raise my eyebrows and make anybody who asked why did I shave my arm feel idiotic. It's a lot simpler to give people a look than get all tangled up in mushy psychoanalysis when it's nobody's business what I do. I rinsed the razor, the shaving cream can and cap, and turned off the water.

Before drying myself, I wiped off all the shaving paraphernalia and shoved it back into the medicine cabinet. Jonas was pounding on the door by the time I was done. "Relax," I said to him on my way out of the bathroom, my towel wrapped around my waist and my smooth arm blocking his passage. He knocked it away, without noticing anything strange, and dashed in fast, muttering under his breath.

The shaved arm itched a little. I considered sneaking into Dad's stuff to get some aftershave, in case that would help, but decided not to risk the potential conversation. I scratched it. Under the red scratch-tracks, it looked a tiny bit more muscular. Zoe and I have been playing a lot of tennis against my garage door, and when I come home, I do twenty-five push-ups and fifty sit-ups; it's possible the arm hair has been hiding muscle tone. *Nice arm,* Zoe might say on the bus this morning. I should think of a comeback, in case.

I pulled on a white cotton T-shirt and my favorite blue shorts, the ones with the hole in the right pocket from my key. I buckled my watch around my wrist and dropped my key into the right pocket, then switched it to the left, which felt weird and unfamiliar. *Maybe I'll put it in my backpack,* I thought, but then, swinging the key around on its long red string, I considered that I'd spend the whole day having mini-panics feeling around inside my right pocket and not finding it, then remembering it was in my backpack. What a time sink. Ever since Mom started working again, I've had this whole key-responsibility stress. I mean, Jonas and I were all for it last year before she started; we were, like, of course, we're old enough to take care of ourselves afternoons, and usually we'll be at whatever practice anyway. It's the key that stresses me, knowing I have to keep track of it, knowing she won't BE here if I fall on my head in the playground or something. They have her work number, of course, and Dad is right down the hill at the high school, but still. The key, my third because I lost the first two, makes holes in my pockets.

I crumpled the string and pushed the key into my right pocket; hole or no hole, I knew I'd be checking for it all day otherwise. It's not that big a hole. As I pulled on my socks, I considered changing into different shorts, but these are my favorites, so I just kept them. My high-tops were by the door. I stepped into them, then slonked down to breakfast, running my hand through my hair. The only good thing about a haircut is you don't have to worry about brushing it for a couple of weeks.

"I can't stand that sound," Mom said without turning around from the counter.

"What sound?" I clomped over toward her.

"Oh! Tie your shoes!" She turned on the coffee-bean grinder. Talk about noise.

I stomped a couple of times.

She hip-checked me. "Wise guy," she muttered.

The thing is, I have this new thing, a habit I guess, that whenever I get a little nervous, my toes grab onto my socks as if my feet are worried I could go tumbling off the earth into orbit if they don't get a tight enough grasp on something. Not nervous like I'm scared or anything. Just, like, when I'm not realizing it, because it happens without my really noticing, until my feet start to cramp. Maybe my feet are bored or something, smooshed up all day in my dark, stinky sneakers, and they want some attention. So anyway, I've been leaving my sneakers untied lately, in hopes maybe my feet will relax if they have more space. It may be because they're growing.

You can't run as fast when your high-tops are untied, Jonas is right, but I wasn't planning to enter any races at the breakfast table. Moving my toes around as I poured myself a bowl of assorted cereals from the boxes lined up on the counter, I agreed with myself again — yup, they definitely look more casual untied, more like I'm not worried about anything.

On the counter beside the cereal boxes were anniversary cards, some from relatives, one from me and Jonas, but a few new ones I hadn't seen yesterday — the kind with extra paper pasted inside, instead of just printing the words right on the cardboard, script writing, some glitter. Romantic stuff to each other, right out on the counter. A pink envelope, torn open, no writing on the front. I pushed it aside with my bowl and caused a card avalanche.

"Tommy," Mom complained.

I sat down at the table and picked up a section of the paper that Dad wasn't reading. "Morning," he said.

"Morning," I answered.

That was about the extent of the conversation until Jonas came charging down. "Had the nightmare again last night," he announced.

"You did?" Mom turned to face him, concerned. "I didn't hear you."

"Tommy came in," Jonas said. "If there really is hell, that's it, I think. Being chased by a windmill."

I tried not to laugh. Dad put down his paper and regarded Jonas in total seriousness. "That's an interesting topic, actually — a person's interpretation of hell."

Oh, spare us, I thought.

Jonas leaned forward in his seat, elbows on the table. "Yeah," he said. "For me it definitely has to do with terror and being chased."

We're going into seventh grade, I thought. *Can we get past the monster stage, please?* I tried to concentrate on eating, keep my mouth full, not start with the sarcasm.

Mom jumped in with a whole thing about what hell it is when people don't talk about their feelings and just try to be polite all the time.

Dad said, "No."

Mom argued, "That's my version; you were just saying it's interesting that people have different perspectives on —"

"That's true," Dad said. "But don't you agree that

true hell would be random violence and results that didn't match causes?"

It is one of the major challenges of my life not to roll my eyes when the man lectures. I concentrated on my cereal. When they all turned to stare at me, I shrugged instead of saying, *This conversation. That's my vision of hell.*

I brought my bowl over to the sink. "We're gonna miss the bus," I told Jonas, leaving the kitchen to search for my books. When I'd gathered them up from the family room and shoved them into my backpack, I called, "'Bye!" with my hand on the front-door doorknob. I was desperate to get out of the house, go be with Zoe, who would never ask my interpretation of hell. Zoe doesn't think about deep issues any more than I do, and her feelings are about as stable as mine are, so you don't have to be all careful.

I heard Jonas scrambling in the kitchen, and then Mom's voice yelling to me, "Wait for your brother, please!" She didn't make him wait for me yesterday. I stomped around a little in the front hall, twisting the doorknob.

"We're gonna miss the bus," I complained, loud.

Mom sighed. "Come back if you do. I'll drive you." She followed Jonas out of the kitchen into the hall, zipping his lunch into his backpack. "You have your inhaler?"

"Yeah," he said, and turned his face up to kiss her.

"He's almost thirteen," I reminded her. "You don't have to ask him every day."

"Ooo!" Mom grabbed Jonas by the face. "Today's the day you find out!"

He nodded. "I think that's why I had the dream last night. I'm so nervous."

"When do you have chorus?"

"Eighth," he groaned.

"Can't you check in earlier and ask?"

Jonas shook his head. "Mrs. Bauman said not to. 'I should know by eighth period,' she said yesterday. I don't think I did that well, though, in the audition."

"We've been over this," Mom told him. "You have the most angelic singing voice and you did great. I heard you. I cried, you sang so beautifully."

I tried not to gag. If I had to hear about Jonas's audition one more time, I might throw up. And each time it's discussed, Mom was more moved by the sheer artistry of his efforts. Soon she'll be saying she literally fainted and had to be given smelling salts. My mother is not a master of understatement.

"Even if I did," Jonas explained, "which I didn't, they only take a few kids out of the hundreds . . ."

Mom wrapped her arms around him. "If they don't want you in that group, then you don't want them."

"They're the best a cappella singing group in Massachusetts. They're semipro," Jonas said. "They sang at the governor's inauguration last year."

"We're gonna miss the bus," I grumbled. We'd been over this territory once or twice before, to say the least. We were about to hear how they were on *Rosie O'Donnell* one time, and Rosie had chatted with the youngest two in the group, one seventh grader and one eighth, asked them if it's hard keeping up with all those older guys, and the seventh grader said as long as he could sing, nothing else bothered him. Rosie called him a cutie-patootie and then gave them all hats. Nana had videotaped it and sent it to us, since Jonas was getting this big honor to audition for them. I thought maybe we could skip over that sweet recollection and actually get to school.

Meanwhile, Dad emerged from the kitchen, unlatching his glasses from his ears. "If you don't make it this year, Jonas, you'll try again next year."

"Maybe," Jonas said. "If I get to. Maybe."

"And even if you don't," Dad quickly answered, recalling I guess that not just anybody can audition; you have to be invited to sing for the prigs. "No matter what happens, at least you know you tried."

"That's right," Mom said, jumping back into the party line. "That's what's important. We're all so proud of you for trying."

"I'm bursting with pride," I said. "Can we go?"

"You know what?" Dad said. "Tell you what. If it's bad news, we'll go bowling to celebrate the courageous putting forth of effort. OK?"

Jonas smiled at him. "OK. Thanks."

"If you never fail, you aren't trying hard enough," Dad said. "Right?"

"Right," Jonas and I said in unison, good soldiers.

"Have a good day," Mom called cheerfully as we pushed out the door into the fresh air.

We tossed our stuff over the fence into Zoe's yard at the same time.

"I thought we were getting out of there before she remembered about today," Jonas said, picking up his books on the other side.

"Yeah, well, fat chance of that," I said, climbing down.

He nodded. "I know it."

"Good luck, though," I offered, slinging my backpack on again.

"I'll need it," he answered. "Thanks. You're so lucky you don't care about anything."

"Yeah," I agreed.

five

It was already there, up ahead, the door closing. It lurched forward. I cursed and sped up. With my high-tops untied, it's hard for me to run fast. The bus's brakes groaned and complained, but Mrs. Horvath, the bus driver, who used to be friends with Mom in high school, opened the doors and sat there fat in her seat, shaking her head at us and waiting. "Don't do us any favors," I mumbled to Jonas, who grunted his agreement, though we both, I know, were grateful she was doing us a favor. The idea of walking back home and begging for a ride to school was a nightmare. Dad would drive us, not Mom, and make us pay by giving us a lecture the whole way there about responsibility and planning and how, when he was a kid, he would've had to walk to school if he missed the bus. Spare us.

So anyway, Jonas was right ahead of me, and I slipped into the seat next to him as the bus groaned into motion. He turned around when Zoe, who was in the row behind us, tapped him on the head and asked if he needed the French homework. I take Spanish. Jonas would never need the French homework, and Zoe knows it. He does it in the afternoon and copies it over, and has it waiting in his little homework folder before he goes to sleep. Did he need the French homework? But Zoe is so sarcastic sometimes. So I realized she was probably teasing him, which made me smile. I was pretty sure Jonas wouldn't get the joke. He is the most sincere person I've ever met.

Jonas turned around, asking, "You're talking to us again?"

I turned to give him a look, like, *Hey, thanks for backing me up when I was saying the same thing*, and noticed his mouth was hanging open as he stared back at Zoe.

"Whoa," he said.

Whoa was right. At least whoa.

Zoe, who normally wears big sweatshirts, was wearing a tight brown top with a little flower printed up at the top center, right above and in between her, well, her, the parts of her body that were bulging out, making small perfect round mounds in the little brown shirt, pulling my eyes toward them like a pair of magnets.

It's not like I've never seen a girl in a tight shirt before, a girl with, you know, a shape. There's this one girl in eighth grade, Carla Obaseki, who has mountains, and her T-shirts are so tight you can see the exact outline of her bra and everything. When she walks down the hall, conversations stop midword, because nobody wants to miss a chance to look.

But Carla Obaseki is a whole different category of girl from Zoe Grandon. Zoe is like one of the guys, a jock, a great girl, with a bright smile and the whitest teeth, and a quick sense of humor and just, you know, somebody you can hang out with all day and bust each other's chops. It's easy, being around her, fun, you feel good about things when you leave, not weird or tense or anything. I've never even said hello to Carla Obaseki, though I did have two dreams about her.

I sunk down in my seat and propped my knees against the green vinyl of the seat ahead of us. My heart was really thumping, and my palms, which tend toward dampness anyway, were absolutely drenched. I braced myself for some comment from Jonas, but he was sitting still as a statue beside me, his face turned toward the window.

From behind us, I heard Zoe's cousin, Gabriela, say something to Zoe, like, "If I had a bust, I'd show it, too." I sank down deeper. Jonas took a deep breath. I almost turned around to tell Gabriela to shut up. It just shows what kind of person Zoe is, that she's so nice to somebody like Gabriela Shaw, who would say a thing like that. Gabriela is huge and gawky and always saying something like that, with a big smile on her face, and who even asked her? She doesn't need to be commenting on people's bodies. No wonder she sits alone at lunch. I mean, I have cousins, but I never feel the need to say body-type words to them. Zoe's been my buddy so long, I'm practically her cousin, too, but you don't hear me saying anything about her body.

I realized I was starting to clench my socks.

I flexed my toes, but then they went right back to digging into the bottoms of my shoes. It occurred to me that my feet might be panicking that I might spring up, turn around, and hang over the back of my seat for another look.

Another look at Zoe? Zoe Grandon, a girl I've seen practically every single day of my entire life. It's not like I was under some delusion that underneath her big, old sweatshirts she was still a seven-year-old. She's four months older than I am. Why would I even want to look at her? There is no reason in the world. *Under-*

neath her sweatshirts. I squeezed my eyes shut and tried to stop thinking those words. *Sing a song,* I told myself — Jonas's trick of how to ignore people — just think of a song and sing it silently in your head. It was hard to think of a single song with *underneath her sweatshirts* pulsing through my mind. *OK,* I told myself, *sing anything. Happy birthday to you, Happy birthday . . .*

I married her at my fifth birthday party. It rained. My mom kept saying all morning, "Maybe it'll hold off." I remember wondering what "hold off" meant. The sky was dark before the guests started showing up; it looked like night. Jonas and I walked around the rented tables on our patio, distributing the juice boxes, but not the paper plates and napkins because of the wind. It smelled damp out there. My father was sweeping the dry leaves off the patio with a big brown broom while Mom ran in and out, taping up decorations and forgetting the chips. Kids started showing up with pairs of presents in their hands, wearing slickers over their costumes. It was getting darker, and the grown-ups each asked my mother if she thought it was going to rain. She kept repeating, "Maybe it'll hold off."

The rain held off long enough for me and Zoe to walk up onto the big rock in my backyard and shrug at each other. My mother was playing a classical finger-picking song on her guitar. Zoe started jumping around, yelling, "We're married, we're married," while her four older sisters and all our friends cheered. I turned to look at Jonas, but he was crying because someone had stepped on his Superman cape and ripped it.

And then a bright explosion of lightning sent us all running for the back door. Zoe lifted her white gauzy dress, exposing the dirt splotches on the knees of her tights, and sprinted past me. My top hat fell off as I ran across the lawn, but when I bent to grab it, the thunder boomed, and, feeling my body begin to shake, I sacrificed the hat to run for safety. Rain was pelting the rainbow-colored streamers hanging from the gutters along the back of the house by the time I got to the back door, so the view out from the dining-room window was of multicolored rain, dripping down into bright puddles on the patio, soaking the unopened juice boxes.

The picture on the cake was smudged, but Jonas and I didn't care because it was Dalmatians anyway, a compromise between my preference of Ernie and Bert, and Jonas's of Superman. Mom had to give out the loot bags early because there wasn't room for the planned relay races inside, and after the cake was devoured, she needed to keep everybody's sugar levels up until three, when their parents slogged up the front steps under umbrellas, to pick them up.

The rain stopped later that afternoon, in time for us to go trick-or-treating. We went with Zoe's family for a little while, and when I stood beside Zoe in her bride's dress, people understood the significance of my father's bow tie hanging limply around my neck and the white Kleenex flower my mother had pinned to the lapel of my jacket, but Jonas and I had just turned five, and so we were accused of slowing down Zoe's older sisters, who were on a mission to get their huge shopping bags stuffed full of candy. The families split ways, and by the third house we hit alone, just the Levits, when I refused to explain — again — what I was supposed to be (A waiter? A man?), my mother announced that Jonas was, obviously, Superman, and that I was Superman's butler, Alfred. "That's Batman's butler," Jonas insisted, but my mother thought the idea was sufficiently hilarious to repeat it at the next few houses. We had to go home then because Jonas lost it, threw himself on somebody's wet lawn, screaming, "Alfred is Batman's butler! It's not funny!" He fell asleep in my father's arms, his eyes swollen from tears and exhaustion. Zoe told me the next day that people all thought she was Cinderella. The next year we had our birthday party on the twenty-seventh, and Zoe and Jonas and I all went as football players for Halloween, which cut down on the confusion.

And that's how it's always been since then, pretty much, me and Jonas and Zoe, the Three Musketeers my mother calls us. I can go into her house almost as easy as into my own. She and my mother have heart-to-hearts, girl stuff. Zoe was the only girl we didn't torture, even in fourth grade. If we had tried chasing her with a stick that had worm blood on it, she'd probably have just beaten us up, or laughed and pretended to eat the worm blood, instead of shrieking and crying. She's about as likely to cry as I am.

It's crazy, is what it is, Zoe in that kind of a sexy-looking shirt. Incongruous. That's the word, the vocab word I got wrong twice last year and had to write a hundred times. Incongruous — doesn't go together. It makes you think of how she looks, which is so not Zoe, that you would think of that. I mean, she has a better arm than most of the boys, including me. In fact, on Labor Day, when there was a cookout at the swim club, she played catch with a bunch of us and she was pretty much the only one who didn't spaz out at all, throw the ball over to where all the cars were, or bounce against the gravel in front of her receiver. I only did that twice, but still, she can get a ball exactly into your palm, every single time. I'm getting worse at throwing lately, the more I practice. Not Zoe; every time, a perfect strike.

Morgan Miller you could see in a tight little T-shirt, definitely imaginable. Oh, yeah. Or even CJ Hurley, who is as flat as me, so nobody would care if she wore a tight shirt. But Zoe? It just didn't make sense, is what was pissing me off. I like things to stay the way they are, not get all screwy without any warning. Like the day I came home in fifth grade, and the kitchen cabinets were painted orange — I was really furious at Mom. Dad thought it was so funny and everything, but it made me feel way off balance. If the kitchen is wood-color when I leave for school, I don't want to come home and find it bright orange; it's not fair. And the same with Zoe wearing a tight little T-shirt.

She was supposed to be the normal thing around here, I thought angrily.

Thank goodness by then we were pulling into the circle at school, so I could get out of that claustrophobic sweaty seat. I've never been so happy to get to school in my life.

six

a bunch of us were hanging around at the lockers, waiting for the bell. I was spacing out, rubbing my hand on the back of my head where it felt practically naked, the hair was cut so short there. I have to stop letting Mom tell the barber what she wants done with my head. It was eighty-something degrees, and the back of my neck was actually cold.

Then I heard Jonas ask if anybody else had noticed the full moon last night. "Jonas is, like, a werewolf," I said, interrupting him. "He's into astrology."

"Astronomy," Jonas corrected.

"Either way." I had been making a joke. I know the difference between astrology and astronomy. My cheeks were hot, everybody looking at me unsure if I'd made a mistake or a joke. I rolled my eyes to let them know. "Ooh, a full moon. Scary."

"It's a scientific fact," my brother was insisting. "Strange things happen when there's a full moon." How can he have no clue at all how to joke back?

"Do we have a math quiz today?" I asked. I was trying to save him, give him a hint to change the subject, since Gideon Weld was standing there smirking at him, encouraging him, waiting for the right opening to humiliate him outright.

"Yeah," Lou Hochstetter said to me. "Word problems." I already knew that. It was only the third day of school; I was still managing to keep track of my assignments, if not completely *do* them.

"And did you see it last night?" Jonas continued, oblivious. "It was so cool-looking, I couldn't stop staring at it."

"So even Jonas the grind might flunk the math quiz, huh?" I smiled at Lou, who grinned back gratefully. Lou is sort of a dork, permanent bed-head, swollen gums from his braces, drops his books a lot, but a nice enough guy. You can always count on him to smile back. "Word problems, huh?"

"No, I studied," Jonas said. "But I couldn't stop staring at the moon."

"Did you spot your home planet?" I smiled, sort of, trying to be still kidding around, trying not to let it look like he was driving me homicidal, wanting to wipe him out of my life before everybody thought I was an annoying weirdo like him, unable to get off the subject of the moon, of all things, when it was so glaringly obvious NOBODY ELSE WAS INTERESTED.

"Huh?" Jonas asked me. If you didn't know him as well as I do, and nobody does, you might think he was just unsure what I meant, or hadn't heard me, but that's not what Jonas meant by *huh*. *Huh* was a threat, behind his blank, calm face.

"Fine," I grunted, clenching my fists. I turned to Gideon and said, "Go for it, Gideon; give him your best shot." Gideon raised his uni-brow and swallowed a bunch of times. His neck is longer than his head.

While Gideon was working on some kind of zinger, Jonas smiled gently, angelically, and said, "The moonlight . . ."

"Shut up!" I yelled.

I should've known that's where he was going. When I was in second grade, I wrote this embarrassing poem about moonlight and loneliness, thinking I was some kind of poetic genius, especially after I read it to Mom, who was blown away by it out of all proportion to its questionable quality. It was just a little-kid rhyme:

> *No one is out walking*
> *No one is out talking*
> *It's bright day, but then*
> *Moonlight strikes again*

Mom acted like I had written the most shockingly haunting, beautiful, original poem in the history of the world. She practically had me convinced, too, so when my second-grade teacher said she thought the poem was "really cute," I cried. I'd brought the poem to school in a special plastic envelope, carried it on my flat palms to present to her like a treasure. *Really cute?* And she thumbtacked it to the bulletin board, beside spelling tests and collages. That night when I told her Mrs. Larkin's reaction, Mom cuddled me up and said some people don't understand poetry. Mom called up my grandmother and had me recite the poem to Nana over the phone, and spent the next few weeks looking through catalogs to find poetry classes for kids who hadn't gotten their grown-up teeth yet. It took me until about the middle of third grade to realize I'm no genius, just because I can rhyme *walk* to *talk*. By then Mom had made me recite that stupid poem to her friends and at family parties, and to the neighbors; I started to notice they all said things like, "That's great. So anyway . . ." Every once in a while Mom will still mention it, like when I get bad marks in English. "You used to be so interested in words, Tommy. Remember that poem. . . ." And Jonas prompts her, "Moonlight, right? I remember that one." He's gotten some good punches for those comments.

So obviously Jonas was just working up to screwing me over in front of our friends, for absolutely no reason, when I'd been protecting him, actually. *Fine then, good, let him try, he'll be sorry.* I braced myself, quickly searching for a comeback. *Yeah, I was into moonlight when I was seven. I used to like Ernie and Bert, too.* But then they might all rag on me about that. No, better to just give him a look like he's not making any sense; the best way to avoid getting mocked is not to put any info out there at all about yourself.

But, of course, Lou and Gideon were now looking back and forth, me to Jonas and back, no clue what we were fighting about. I opened my hands, like, *Come on, now, try to hit me, you coward.*

Jonas flashed me a quick smile and said, "I read this thing that said strange occurrences really do happen during a full moon."

"Yeah?" Lou asked tentatively, still shifting his eyes

between me and my brother. My fists were tight again, ready.

"Not like people turning into werewolves," Jonas whispered. "But seriously, more women deliver babies, and more crimes are committed. I read it in the paper."

"Oh, that proves it," Gideon Weld said, his elbow digging into my side. He tries to be sarcastic, but he fails. I stepped away from him. Gideon wants to be Mr. Witty, Mr. Tough Guy, and that's the best he can come up with? Skepticism about the accuracy of the press?

I squinted at him. "What kind of stupid are you?"

He looked insulted. Good.

"Really," Jonas insisted. "It was in *The New York Times*."

That cracked Gideon up. There was no way I could save Jonas from such a stupid comment. Lou and I laughed, too. It was sort of a relief.

But then Gideon stammered, mid-laugh, trying to catch his breath, "You, you, you SMELL like you read *The New York Times*."

Lou and I stopped laughing and blinked at Gideon, who was left laughing his high-pitched laugh all alone. As his laughter died down and he began to look pleadingly at us, me, Jonas, and Lou broke out laughing. "Weak," I managed to say. "Even for you, Gideon."

Jonas tilted his head to the side and asked, "How would that smell, anyway, Gideon?"

I thought Lou was gonna wet his pants.

"Like you, that's how," Gideon said, pretending he was only pretending to be angry. "Like farts, fart-head."

All four of us were just about dying of hysterics at that point, when Zoe turned the corner and walked toward us in that tight little shirt of hers. She was surrounded by a gang of girls, but we all stared right at her, at her chest.

Jonas blinked a few times and shook his head. Jonas doesn't even like girls, or at least he hasn't ever tried to kiss one or anything. He just goes along, humming his own little made-up tunes, staring out windows at the moon, and then telling the guys, practically bragging about it, without any clue what a geek he sounds like. It's weird he doesn't get beat up more, especially with his rosy cheeks and long eyelashes. Guys know they'll have to take me on, too, if they push too far with him — two for the price of one, Gideon complained last year, after I'd knocked the wind out of him and put out my hand to help Jonas up. But even angelic Jonas was staring at Zoe's chest.

Zoe's eyes were lasered on the floor, her arms entwined with other girl-arms. They walked past us like a moving wall or an army. I felt my cheeks getting hot again, and my palms were practically dripping sweat, though the back of my neck still felt frosty.

After the girls passed and it was only their backs, their safe backs, we could see, Lou cleared his throat and said, "Full moon, huh?" His voice cracked.

"Very full," I said. I chewed on my bottom lip, thinking about it. Who knows? It sounds like a load of crap to me, but if it really was in the paper, maybe there was something to it. People were definitely acting weird. And something felt sort of off inside me, too, something even beyond the palm waterworks and the foot cramps — so maybe it was just a moon thing. Jonas reads the "Science Times" section.

I started following Zoe and the other girls, feeling cocky and relieved it was the moon's fault everybody was freaking out. At least that explained it.

"What are you gonna do?" Gideon Weld whispered, juggling his precariously balanced pile of books. He got them under control and tapped me. "What are you gonna do?"

"Zap her," I answered quickly, to shut him up.

"Do it," he said, keeping up with me and rubbing that stubble on his chin. "Yeah, do it!"

I reached toward Zoe and grabbed the bulge of bra strap in the middle of her back. I stopped walking and, after she took another step, let go. It thwacked against her back.

Zoe ducked her head. The girls mumbled to one another, but didn't really react. So I did it again: grabbed her bra strap and zapped her with it. Their step quickened; they pulled tighter together. I sped up, too. I couldn't stop then, could I? I was grinning like an idiot, I realized, my face frozen into this tight jack-o'-lantern mask. *React already, would you?* I grabbed for her bra strap again, but before I could get a grip, Zoe spun around.

All of us stopped moving. Zoe pushed her lower jaw forward and stared at me with the angriest look in her eyes. She's a tiny bit taller than I am, so I had to tilt my head up embarrassingly to meet her stare. Couldn't stop smiling, though it occurred to me she was about to beat the living crap out of me. I couldn't even coordinate my fingers into fists to fight back, just stood there smiling like an idiot while she narrowed her blue eyes at me, willing myself not to break the staring contest to sneak a peek at her shirt.

She turned away.

Just totally dissed me, in front of everybody. I had been braced for her fists or some wisecrack, at least, but she just gives me a look and stalks away, like, I'm not even worth her time? What's with her lately? Can't she take a joke? Man, if she loses her sense of humor, too, I'm gonna be so alone.

Gideon Weld shoved me toward her. I tripped forward and, to stop myself from crashing into her, went for that bra strap, so clearly outlined under the tight brown cotton stretched across Zoe's back, and prepared to zing her into tomorrow.

She spun around so fast I backed up a step onto Gideon's foot, but Zoe's finger was in my face, closer to my eyes than the tip of my nose is. She leaned in so close I could smell her toothpaste. Mint.

She said, "If you touch me again, I'll rip off your thing and staple it to your head."

seven

I got to homeroom somehow. I'm not sure how. I remember swallowing a fair amount and not saying anything to anyone. The halls seemed unusually quiet or maybe it was my head exploding that overwhelmed the usual school noises. *Rip off your . . .*

I sunk down into my chair, then changed my mind, shifted backward, and rested my head on my crossed arms on the desk.

Staple it to my head? Where did she get that?

I felt a tap on my shoulder. I guess I was a little on edge because that tap startled me so much I jumped. My knees hit the desk; my books slid off. When I tried to grab them, I got only a corner of my loose-leaf.

The bulk of it flipped over and dumped my assignment pad out and onto the floor. I let go of the loose-leaf and grabbed for the assignment pad. It's the one thing I DON'T need anybody seeing inside of.

"Sorry," Gabriela said, towering over me and smiling. She crouched down and closed my loose-leaf.

"Don't!"

She backed away a little. "Sorry," she said again, sympathetically.

"It's OK."

She smiled, as if this were an invitation, and stepped closer, close enough to rest her fingers on my desk. "Did, are you OK?"

"I'm fine!" I finished gathering up my things, folded my arms protectively on top of them, and let my head drop again. Her fingers were an inch from my eyes. I noticed she chews her fingernails and cuticles, same as I do, leaving the same jagged, swollen red areas. I closed my eyes. Just who I need to be like.

"You want to be left alone?" she asked.

I didn't answer. How obvious was it I wanted to be left alone? I know I shouldn't be nasty to Gabriela, of all people. She's always so well-meaning and cheerful it nauseates me, makes me crabby like too little sleep. If my parents were going through a divorce and everybody in Boggs knew it, like with Gabriela's parents —

if I were living half-time in my house and half-time in an apartment down on Bromley Road, I wouldn't be cheerful the way she is. She was over at Zoe's fairly often this past year while her parents were sorting things out. (That's what Gabriela said, "My parents are sorting things out, so I'm here again, sorry.") Zoe never said anything, not to me anyway, never defended her cousin when I groaned, never complained about her when Mrs. Grandon sent Gabriela outside to hang with us. Zoe just included her. One time we let her play tennis with us against my garage door, and she accidentally smacked Zoe across the jaw with her racquet, and Zoe had to go to the hospital and get eight stitches in her chin. Gabriela cried a lot, but Zoe didn't. She kept saying it didn't even hurt, don't worry, it's fine, be an improvement on my face, probably. As her dad searched for the car keys and his shoes to drive her to the emergency room, Zoe stood there in my driveway laughing and joking, reassuring her cousin, smiling above the blood soaking through my mother's towels.

Zoe.

The final bell rang. I listened to the squealing of chairs as people grabbed them and dove in. Our homeroom teacher, Mrs. Shepard, told us the first day that you get marked late if you're not actually in your seat when the final bell for homeroom rings, and Mrs. Shepard is not famous for joking. Everybody calls her The Sadist, in fact. She teaches seventh-grade English and social studies, too, and in the two days I've had her so far it's become clear to me that she is not someone whose buttons you want to press. She was probably the kind of girl who wouldn't have stood for boys snapping her bra strap when she was in seventh grade, either.

I lifted my head. Mrs. Shepard was staring at me as if she could tell I was imagining her bra strap, which I wasn't, not really, I'm not that perverted; Mrs. Shepard is like a hundred years old. Her eyebrows were raised into little tepee triangles above her pale blue eyes, and her pointy tongue lightly touched the bottom edge of her upper lip. My ears felt hot. I held on to the seat of my chair with both hands until Mrs. Shepard's eyebrows relaxed and she shifted her gaze elsewhere.

I opened my assignment pad as inconspicuously as possible while the announcements started on the PA. I just needed something to do with my fidgety hands, to keep from chewing on the cuticles. I pulled one of my new pens out of my pencil holder at the front of my loose-leaf, darting glances at Mrs. Shepard to make sure she wasn't about to nail me. She was leaning on the edge of her desk, arms crossed over her broad chest, surveying us suspiciously. But not particularly me.

When I looked down at my pad, I saw the Z I had doodled there.

I erased it quickly, before anyone could see. What a mess, and I don't only mean the ink that wouldn't erase completely. What if Jonas was right yesterday? What if I have a crush on Zoe Grandon?

Oh, man. That would totally suck.

The Z wouldn't erase. Its ghost was there on the page no matter how many times I rubbed it out, no matter how much of the eraser I used up. What a girly thing, doodling her initial. What is wrong with me? It all started with these stupid pens — erasable pens. That's a wimpy attitude right there, like you might want to take back what you write. I can write a Z if I want. Maybe I was starting to write ZERO. Subconsciously. Since I am a total ZIP lately. Maybe I was going to write ZEBRA for some reason. Who says I can't write ZEBRA if I want to write ZEBRA?

Still a shadow of the Z, and Mrs. Shepard started to look suspicious of my energetic erasing. That's it. I'm bringing these wimpy loser pens back to Sundries, demand my money back. Erasable pens. What's the point? They smudge so much more than other pens, I have splotches of blue up the side of my writing hand, and still you can't erase a single simple letter Z if you don't want to see it in ink in front of you. That's it, I'm getting my money back. I ripped out the paper from my assignment pad and crumpled it.

Mrs. Shepard's eyebrows went triangular in my direction again. I tried to make my face as neutral as possible. *Calm, calm. Don't ask for trouble, Tommy, lay low.* When anything upsets Jonas, he cries; everybody sees, everybody knows. Same if he's feeling happy — he still hugs Mom and kisses her, even sometimes in front of people. Not me. I haven't let her kiss me in front of people since kindergarten. *Mr. Tough Guy,* Mom says, but I can't help it if that's the way I am.

After a few seconds, Mrs. Shepard looked over at Gabriela, who had shifted in her seat. *Thank you, Gabriela,* I thought, and resolved to be nicer to her, in gratitude.

So what if I do have a crush on Zoe? A small crush. Nobody has to know. Not her, not Jonas, nobody. Stay neutral and nobody will find out. Last time I liked a girl it was a total disaster, and Morgan wasn't even my friend, so there wasn't anything to lose, going out with her. It was sort of nice for a little while, actually, having a girlfriend, but then when we finally hooked up, one day when she came over and kissed me out in my tree house, it was not so nice. I kind of freaked out and ran away from her into my house. I was getting a virus anyway, which probably contributed to the chaos of the moment, but seriously, she out of the blue was making out with me, her face smooshed into mine, before I even realized what was going on, and I had to push her away and run. I had 103 for three days, and weird, weird dreams — hallucinations that the small print in the front of the book I was reading revealed secrets, like, that Abraham Lincoln never particularly wanted to free the slaves (don't know why that freaked me out so much, but trust me, at the time I was completely terrified that I had this information), and that the mitten I had lost wasn't really lost but was being kept for evidence by some evil spy ring whose operatives dressed as clowns and used plungers as weapons. I think the toilet might've been stopped up at the same time, so maybe I got confused, seeing our decrepit old plumber wandering past my door, felt paranoid about what he was going to do to me with that plunger slung over his shoulder like an ax. I had some chase dreams, too, though I was being chased by Nazis, not by a windmill, and I think I ended up saving the whole town. By time that I was getting better, Mom wasn't coming in my room to check on me as often, bringing me cups of water and pushing the hair off my forehead to test the fever there with her lips. I can't say I minded it totally, letting myself sleepily relax into being taken care of like that, and, of course, I got to miss a bunch of days of school, which I usually don't get away with. I never even get a cold, usually. Our pediatrician calls me *Jonas's lost twin* when I come in for my annual checkup, since he only sees Jonas, in between, for his asthma flair-ups and allergic reactions and bronchitis and whatever else he comes down with. But as nice as it was to be the vulnerable one, cuddled and coddled for a change, it wore thin by the third day, and I promised myself I was not rushing into liking a girl again in the near future. Maybe I have an allergy, too, after all, and it's girlfriends. If Jonas eats a walnut, he could die.

Not that Zoe is anything like a walnut, or even like Morgan Miller. Zoe would never try to kiss me.

I was having a serious problem with temperature — I couldn't decide if I was freezing or broiling. I wiped the sweat off my forehead into my hair, but the skin on my face was cold and clammy. *Don't think about it,* I told myself. Nobody knows and nobody has to know. If I could just stop thinking about Zoe and me kissing, out in my tree house. Kissing Zoe?

Thirteen times table. Thirteen times two is twenty-six. Thirteen times three is thirty-nine. Not helping.

Still thinking about kissing. She's my buddy, practically my cousin, so there is NO REASON for my body to be doing all this freaking out. Didn't my body used to be under my control? I used to be able to throw a ball where I intended it to go, and I could sit at my desk and not be in a total panic that if the bell rings now, I can't get up without everybody knowing exactly what is going on with me. Thirteen times four is . . .

Like I care in the slightest what thirteen times four is. My father's advice. *If you need to get your mind off something, calm your body down, I, well, guys, it always works for me to do times tables or the presidents. Word to the wise.* Jonas and I talked about it that night, after Dad had that little man-to-man-to-man chat with us. So far that's all he's told us about sex or girls or becoming a man. Neither of us had any idea what he meant. Or at least neither of us admitted any idea to each other. *Name the presidents? Thanks, Dad.* I had an idea what Dad was hinting at, I guess, but in case Jonas didn't, I pretended to be as clueless as he was. But that was last year. *Washington, Adams, Jefferson, Madison, Monroe, Adams . . .*

I held the crumpled notepaper lightly in my hand until the bell rang, then counted to five before I stood up — don't need to attract Mrs. Shepard's attention or anybody else's, though my body had calmed down. OK, I guess. *Thanks, Dad.* Nothing like dead presidents to kill a buzz. I shoved my books back into my backpack and tossed the wad of paper with the erased Z into the wastepaper basket on my way to the classroom door.

"You sure you're OK?" Gabriela asked me on our way out the door.

I gave her a puzzled look, like what's wrong with *you?*

"No, because you look a little greenish," she said, holding the door for me. "And, I don't mean to pry but, is one of your arms hairier than the other?"

eight

"Zoe really got you!" Gideon said, body-slamming me sideways.

I kept walking toward Spanish, after a slight stumble. Really got me how? I didn't want to ask him. Be cool, say nothing.

"Ooo, Zoe got Tommy!" he chanted.

"You ever wash your hair, Gideon?" I sped up. "Or at least get the oil changed?"

"King of comebacks, huh?" Gideon raked the long, greasy hair out of his eyes. "She threatens to rip out your private parts, and what did you say to her? Maybe I missed part of what you said, you were running down the hall away from her so fast."

"Take a bath." I pushed past him into Spanish and headed up the aisle toward my seat.

"Oh, that's a good one, too. 'Take a bath.' Hmm, I'd say that's weak, even for you, Tommy."

"*¿Hay un problema, amigos?*" asked Mr. Ramos, the student teacher in Spanish. I didn't answer. I lifted the lid of my desk, slipped my backpack inside, and got into the attached chair. I hate these desks, the one-piece kind with the chair strung up to the desk by a metal pole. You can't tilt back.

"She burned you bad," Gideon added, pressing his luck as he folded his long, flabby body into the seat next to mine. "If you ask me, you should've . . ."

"Yeah, Gideon," I lashed out. "You're just the one I'll ask for advice about girls."

"*¿Problemas con chicas?*" Mr. Ramos asked, sauntering up the aisle toward me and Gideon. Great, Gideon, thanks a lot, just what I need. A teacher involved. He stopped at my desk and asked, "*¿Que pasó?*"

Right, sure, let me lay out my personal problems here in the middle of first period — well, see, *Señor* Ramos, there's this girl I may be falling in love with, and she wants to tear off my you-know-what and staple it to my head, I ticked her off so bad. But wait, let me try to tell it to you in Spanish. Yeah. Maybe I'll get back to you on that one. "Um, *nada*," I managed to say.

He didn't get the hint right away. He hovered there at my desk for a minute, waiting. Ramos isn't even a teacher yet, not till next year. He's just supposed to be learning by helping out *Señora* Goldsmith, who I guess is planning to cut Spanish every Friday and leave us to him alone. When she introduced him the first day as "*Señor* Ramos," he looked about ready to crack up; I bet nobody's ever called him *Señor* before. He's way cooler-looking than old Goldsmith, that's for sure, with his black hair curling over his collar and his shiny shoes and matching belts, thin linen shirts crisply ironed and loosely tucked over tight tank tops. I looked up at him. He was watching me — not in a threatening way, though he was definitely flexing, no teacher's biceps are that big just relaxing — but like he sort of knew what was going on. He flashed me a microsmile and then, to my relief, turned away and walked back up to the front of the classroom.

Maybe I should stay for a minute after class, talk to him. You always hear it's a good idea to find an adult you can confide in, a mentor, when you have problems. Mr. Ramos is probably the coolest man I know, now that I think of it — who was I supposed to ask how to act if you think you might seriously like a girl — Jonas? Gideon? Dad? Yeah, maybe he could give me some more helpful tips. Capitals of the states? There's only so far you can go with that type of advice.

CJ Hurley walked up the left aisle toward me, her head bowed. She was wearing that tight bun I'd been accused of mocking yesterday. I honestly have nothing against a bun or any other hairstyle. Zoe wears hers in a ponytail when she's playing sports, and I like the way it sways behind her when she runs. It's nice just long and loose like Zoe normally wears it, also, but there's nothing wrong with a bun.

The thing is, I don't care about girls' hair. Not at all, not one single bit. Why would I make fun of a girl's hair? Or even notice it? What a ridiculous idea, I was making fun of CJ's bun. Like I would even think enough about a girl's hairstyle to make fun of it. I was just trying to make conversation, nothing more than that. A person can't say anything without everybody acting all suspicious.

I glared at CJ, feeling suddenly furious that she'd obviously made a big deal to Zoe about a totally nothing comment about her hair, but she was staring straight ahead. She has an interesting walk — sort of a cross between a duck, because her feet point away from each other, and a cat, her steps so quiet and light. There is something distant and removed about her, I guess because she has a talent. I wonder how that must feel, to know when you're only twelve what you're good at and meant to be already. I get the feeling that she's really *deep*.

She glanced at me and caught me looking. I started to smile pleasantly at her, but she frowned.

I flicked my eyes away so she wouldn't think I was staring at her. Which I wasn't. A person's eyes have to be somewhere, right?

One of these days it would be cool to talk to her about ballet. Personally I don't get it; I fell asleep last year when we went to see her in *The Nutcracker,* but still I think it might be interesting to hear what it's like to be, like, a prodigy, gifted, special. Then again, she'd probably think I was teasing her or something. And the guys would accuse me of having a crush on her. Forget it. I don't want to know that bad.

Morgan Miller scurried up the aisle after CJ, grabbed her elbow, and whispered to her before CJ had a chance to sit down, Morgan's hand cupped over CJ's little pale ear. When she was done, they both turned slightly toward me. I was still there, right next to them, trapped in my seat. I gave up on trying to find somewhere else to look and stared at them instead. *You have a problem with me?* Morgan grabbed CJ and whispered some more secrets to her.

Wimps.

I forced myself not to chew on my cuticles but instead to sit there, not move, be cool, be tough. This is what I meant when I told Zoe the other day that she's more like one of the guys. You wouldn't catch her dead, whispering and peeking out the corner of her eyes, the way CJ and Morgan do.

No, just a good quick kick to where it hurts. *Staple it to my head?*

Meanwhile, Mr. Ramos leaned against his desk and waited for the bell to ring, looking slightly amused at whatever thought he was thinking. I imagined approaching him after class: *Mr. Ramos — could I ask you a question? It's about a girl.*

The bell rang. Mr. Ramos didn't move. We all watched him expectantly. Slowly, slowly, he smiled. "Put your books away, *mis amigos*," he said. "And get ready for your first surprise quiz of the year."

Just what I needed. I knew I should've looked at those vocab words last night during commercials. Super. All around me people were groaning. I wished I could go back to bed and start the whole day over. That's what my four-year-old cousin Zachary says, when he gets cranky and overwhelmed or can't have his way: *Now we have to start the whole day over, from dawn!*

My books were already away, in my backpack in my desk, so I just sat there. By habit my fingers checked my right pocket, for my key.

Not there.

I sat up straight. Mr. Ramos was handing out the quiz sheets. The key wasn't in my other pocket, either.

I tried to think what I'd done with it. I remembered thinking about where to put it, diddling with it in my room as I got ready for school. Did I put it in my backpack? Shoot. It definitely wasn't in either pocket. This time I have to pay for a replacement, Dad said so last time I lost my key. I don't know why I can't keep track of my things. It really makes Dad angry. He looks at me like I'm unrecognizable to him when I lose something, and tells me, "I'm a reasonable man, but . . ." Whenever he tells me he's a reasonable man, I always think, *That must be a nice thing to know about yourself.* I'm smart enough not to say it out loud.

I'm so dead, I thought. I am not a reasonable man. I am — what am I? Well, a mess. I am — falling apart. I am . . .

Maybe it's in my backpack?

A sheet of paper breezed onto my desk. I glanced at it. Looked at the first word. Never seen it before in my life. Great, just great. I rested my hot, cold head in my palms, trying to squeeze something out of my brain manually. Don't panic.

The house is locked and if I need to get in, I can't. Jonas has his key, of course, Mr. Perfect wouldn't have lost his, but what if I wanted to get in without him, by myself? My own house. I should be able to get into my own house.

And these words are in a foreign language!

Relax, I told myself, but I didn't listen. Maybe the key is in my backpack. Do the quiz, then look.

I checked the bottom vocab word on the list. Number twenty. Never seen it before, either. In a full-body sweat, I closed my eyes tight. OK, this is a nightmare. *Windmill Man.* In Jonas's nightmare, he's walking down a beautiful dirt road in bright sunshine, acres of flowers on either side, humming a song he made up, feeling all happy, until he feels someone, or some-*thing* I guess, behind him. He starts to walk faster, straighter. The sky darkens a little. He speeds up more but doesn't run. *Be calm,* he says he tells himself. *Don't run.* He tries to keep humming, but he can't get the tune anymore and meanwhile he hears Windmill Man getting closer, feels him. The *whir-whir-whir* noise gets overwhelmingly loud, and that's when Jonas starts to run.

Turn around and face him, I've told Jonas, but he says while he's in the dream he can't. One time he said he wished I could come into the dream with him, to protect him, but I can't. When he feels the whirring arms of the Windmill Man scraping him, he screams, and it's the sound of his screams, he says, that wakes him up, and he finds himself soaked in sweat, shaking and terrified, but safe in his bed.

Last night in my bed, after I got him the water and stuff, waiting for my mother's footsteps to come down the hall and comfort him, I imagined, *What if it were me?* What if I were the one with the heart-pounding, sheet-drenching drama of feeling defenseless, pursued, exposed? And then waiting to be rescued. I fell asleep trying to conjure the Windmill Man for myself, but I didn't dream anything.

And yet here I was in Spanish class, shaking and sweating, in the midst of my own nightmare. Nobody's on her way down the hall with a towel for me, though, I reminded myself.

I crossed one arm over the front of my desk and slipped the other under it, into the dark cool inside. Forced my eyes to stay steady on my Spanish quiz, without really focusing on it. I just knew that if I could locate my key, I'd be able to get going on the stupid Spanish quiz. Spanish Inquisition. I unzipped the front pocket of my backpack and reached inside, among the pencils and lint.

The desk slammed down hard on my arm.

"Ow!"

Mr. Ramos's muscular hand was pressing the lid of my desk into my forearm. Without letting up on the pressure at all, he asked, "What do you think you're doing?"

Amputation was the only word I could think of. A noise escaped from me that sounded depressingly like a whimper. *Be tough*, I begged myself.

"I don't tolerate cheating in my class," Mr. Ramos said.

"I'm not," I said, thinking, *It's not even your class.* "I swear. I wasn't."

He eased up the pressure just enough to let me whip my arm out of there. There was an angry red indentation across it, which I rubbed. Didn't help. Jonas would ask to go to the nurse, I thought. Or cry. Not me. I sniffed hard and forced myself to stop rubbing. I squinted up at Mr. Ramos and said, "I was just checking to make sure I have my house key."

I have to admit, it was a much tougher and more reasonable-sounding explanation when I tried it inside my head.

Mr. Ramos turned my quiz, saw I hadn't filled in a single answer, and spun it back to face me.

"I swear," I repeated.

He went back up the aisle toward his desk without beating me up or sending me to the office. While his back was to me, I turned and smirked at CJ Hurley, who I could feel watching me, to show her I wasn't intimidated by the teacher. She looked quickly away, and as I watched her, I could see her shaking her head slightly on its long, skinny neck.

I wiped my sweaty hands off on my shorts and picked up my pen again. The words were still foreign.

Surprise quizzes are so unfair. If they want to test us, fine, but a little warning seems like a reasonable requirement. At least, let us prepare. Things should be what you expect, or else it's just trying to trap innocent people.

nine

I made a couple of guesses, a few reasonable stabs based on similar-looking words in English, left a bunch blank. So much for doing well this year. I kept my eyes on my feet as I walked to the front, slapped my quiz onto the top of the pile, and went back to my seat, choosing the aisle on Gideon's side rather than CJ's and Morgan's.

As soon as I was back in my seat, which I had to climb into this time, having gone up the wrong aisle and therefore encountering the steel bar barricade, I opened my desk all the way — yes, Mr. Ramos, I really was looking in my backpack for my KEY — and yanked out my bag. Unzipped the pocket and rummaged around. No.

I let the bag drop on the floor and left the desk flipped open until Ramos made me close it, then spent the rest of the period numbing out. I barely noticed the bell ringing, and, in fact, it wasn't until everybody was scrambling out the door that I snapped out of it and picked up my stuff. I noticed among the other scribbles on the board there was a homework assignment. Oh, well. Not planning to stop, take out my loose-leaf and assignment pad at that point. Deal with that later.

The key still wasn't in my pockets, no matter how many times I checked. I trudged down the hall toward Ms. Cress's for math/science. The tingly feeling, the excitement and anger and even the humor of what had happened with Zoe before homeroom was gone. 9:19 in the morning and I was already exhausted. I just wanted to find Jonas, make sure he had his key.

I walked past Gideon to where Jonas was standing, right outside Ms. Cress's. "You have your key?"

Jonas nodded, and then his eyes narrowed a tiny bit. "What?" he asked quietly.

I looked down and away, not wanting him to see anything was wrong. *Not now,* I thought, or bargained. *Deal with it later. Please don't ask more,* I begged him silently.

"Here comes your girlfriend," Gideon announced,

and without thinking I lifted my head. Zoe, red-faced and tight-shirted, was passing us, ducking into the room. "Another good comeback!" Gideon cheered.

"Give it a rest," Jonas said to him. "Come on, Tommy." He turned and walked into the classroom.

I followed him, leaving Gideon in the hall alone.

Zoe was sinking into her chair. I didn't want to get too close, so I stayed right behind my brother, like he was blocking for me. Kept my head down and fell into Jonas's walking rhythm, right, left, letting him set the pace across the front of the classroom. Let him take on the defense for once.

Following him up the row toward our seats, though, I gave him a shove on the back of his shoulder. It didn't budge him much, scrawny as he is. He walked another step or two, then stopped. Waited.

"I don't need you to defend me, you know," I whispered.

He placed his books on his desk. "OK," he said.

"What do you mean, OK?" I demanded.

Jonas didn't answer.

"You think I DO need your help? Suddenly?"

Jonas sat down in his chair and watched me. He looked calm, but a little, I thought, amused.

I kicked the leg of his chair. "What?"

"Pretty bothered, huh?"

"By what?"

"By *what*?" he repeated, and cocked his head back toward Zoe. "Ouch."

"Oh, that?" I tried to sound surprised, like I hadn't given it another thought. "What do I care? She thinks she's so tough?" I said it loud enough so Zoe had a chance to hear, if she was listening. I didn't want her to think I was making a big deal.

"She seems pretty tough to me," Jonas said, leaving himself wide open.

"To you, maybe."

He smiled up at me, that angelic smile that makes Mom echo-smile but makes me want to punch his straight teeth.

"I already forgot all about it," I lied. "You mean what she said this morning? Lame. Can't even remember what she said." I didn't have the guts to glance over at her and see if any of this was registering.

"Sure, sure. You forgot," Gideon butted in. "You want a reminder? Hey, Zoe!"

Jonas stood up in front of Gideon and asked him, "Was somebody talking to you, Gideon?" Like I need Jonas of all people standing up to Gideon Weld on my behalf. As if I'm the one who's all vulnerable and scared. Let him try to take care of himself — I can handle my own life, thank you very much. He was flexing his nonexistent muscles, his face serious but questioning, tilted up to stare into Gideon's. I felt weirdly left out.

Jonas turned slowly from Gideon and faced me, to ask, "So what happened to your key?"

"Don't know," I admitted. "It was right here, and now, I don't know. It disappeared." I hated how wimpy I sounded. As if Jonas were the one who could send me to my room or tell me he's disappointed in me.

Jonas shrugged. "Full moon."

What I didn't need right then, with Zoe and her little girlfriends all probably watching me get humiliated for the second time in one morning, was for Jonas to first defend me like I'm some weakling pathetic baby and then to start mocking me with his full-moon baloney, as if I'm the one who believes in that crap. "Yeah, right," I said. "That must be it. The full moon, or maybe Windmill Man got it."

"What's Windmill Man?" Gideon asked.

Jonas didn't say anything. He sat down.

"What's Windmill Man?" Gideon asked again. "Can I download it from you?"

"Ask Jonas," I croaked, and went to my seat.

Gideon looked at Jonas. "Where did you get it?"

"I have bad dreams sometimes," Jonas said quietly. "A windmill chases me and tries to kill me."

Ms. Cress rushed into class and started chatting fast and furious. The speed of the earth around its axis, and around the sun — she sounded honestly fascinated with her own story. "I'll show you the calculation," she bubbled, and spun around in her high-heeled boots to go to the board. "Anybody see chalk? Where's the chalk?"

She yanked the drawer out of her metal desk and ruffled through whatever was in there. "Nothing!" She slapped her legs. "How weird is this?"

"Full moon," I mumbled.

Gideon laughed. I sunk down lower in my seat. Sometimes I hate myself.

"What was that?" Ms. Cress asked, more interested than harsh.

Jonas turned around to look at me questioningly. I ducked my head. Screw him. He asks for it. He has no idea how much, how often I protect him, and then he acts like this.

Nobody answered Ms. Cress. "Well," she said, sighing. "Would somebody go to the office for me and get some chalk?"

Just about every hand in the room went up.

"Wow. What a helpful bunch this year! OK, um, you can go." She pointed at Jonas. "Are you Thomas or Jonas?"

"I'm Jonas," said Jonas. We look nothing alike. People just sometimes keep us in the Levit Twins section of their heads, I think, and can't be bothered remembering which is me and which is him. I lowered my shaved arm, watching him go. I felt weighed down with sorry-for-myself.

As Ms. Cress continued talking about how fast the earth was spinning, I found myself gripping the edges of my desk. I could feel the earth spinning, I swear it. It felt like being on a roller coaster. Both my feet cramped. The middle toe on my right one sprung straight out and low, which made me jolt upright in my chair and kick off my shoe, to massage it.

"Something wrong?" Ms. Cress asked me.

"No!" I stomped on the floor to get rid of the spasm, but it didn't go.

"OK," said Ms. Cress. "Why don't you all take out your homework and we'll go over it until Thomas, I mean Jonas, comes back with the chalk. We started discussing the calculation of how fast the earth turns on its axis yesterday. Right?"

A few people mumbled, a few people grumbled. The noise of opening notebooks and flipping papers drowned out her voice.

". . . used to think the reason it takes longer one way than the other if you go between here and Europe on a plane was because of the earth's rotation, right? You following me?"

Barely, I thought, massaging my freaking-out foot and flipping to my mess of science homework, half-done.

"Did any of you think that?"

A couple of the girls up toward the front raised their hands sheepishly. Brownnosers.

"Right. But I said something about that to a friend of mine who's a meteorologist," Ms. Cress continued, thrusting one hip out to the side and resting a fist on it. "He laughed at me. 'No! The atmosphere turns with the earth.' And I was confused, honestly. I started to argue with him, 'The air? Turns with the earth?'"

She had on a thumb ring. On the hand resting on her hip, in her short skirt. I think it's distracting for a teacher to wear a thumb ring.

"My friend couldn't believe I didn't understand. He said, 'Think about it — otherwise what would the wind speed be when you walked out your door? Life would be totally unsustainable.'"

She grinned triumphantly at us. I don't know if anybody else was making sense of her revelations. I was too unbalanced by my foot spasms and her thumb ring, not to mention everything else. I thought, *Life IS totally unsustainable.*

"And he was absolutely right." Ms. Cress lifted her hands into the air. "Which shows once again how math formulas are so relevant!"

Jonas walked into the room with a fresh box of chalk. Ms. Cress turned the full wattage of her toothpaste-commercial smile on him and said, "Perfect timing! Gimme!"

He handed her the chalk box warily.

"Excellent," Ms. Cress enthused. "I love a fresh box of chalk, don't you?"

Nobody answered. We all just stared at her as she began making notes on the board with a long, squawking piece of chalk.

As he walked up the aisle toward his seat, Jonas tilted his head at me and put on this concerned expression, like the one Mom gives him when he coughs. I stomped my foot again, and though my toe was still pointing stubbornly south, shoved it back into my shoe. Jonas sucked in on his lips. When he got to his seat, he whispered, "You OK?"

I kicked his chair with my convulsed foot and grunted, "I don't need your help!"

ten

Zoe walked toward me, across the crowded, chaotic cafeteria, her squad of friends massed tightly behind her. Her hair was weird, different. It took me the whole time she was heading over to our table to figure out what it was — there were pens stuck through it in the back, holding it off her neck in a sort of a bun, but not neat like CJ's. Sort of a mess, actually. Her arms were crossed over her chest and she was hunched forward, as if someone had just knocked the wind out of her. Her mouth was hanging slightly open, so I could see her tongue flicking around inside.

When she got to the opposite side of our lunch table, she stopped. Gideon had already stood up to throw out his crumpled lunch bag and the peanut-buttery Baggie inside it, but he stopped and waited beside me, crinkling the brown paper in my ear. I watched his hands on the bag, to avoid having to look up at the girls who were standing across from us, waiting.

"Um," Zoe said.

I looked up at her. I had no other choice. I had no idea what was about to happen, one of my least favorite feelings in the world. My right leg started to shake, so I was pretty psyched I was still sitting, my legs hidden under the table. I didn't need anybody thinking I was nervous from some girl saying "um" to me.

"Sorry," she said.

If I had to rank the top one hundred possible things I thought she'd say to me, "sorry" wouldn't have been anywhere near the list.

"For what?" I asked her.

"For threatening to rip off your, you know, thing."

Well, I suppose I asked for that. Gideon and Lou and maybe some other guys were laughing, behind me. I punched Gideon's soft belly and enjoyed the feeling, my fist thunking into it.

I took a deep breath and then, mustering only half my courage, looked up at Zoe with one eye, the other squinted closed. She was smirking. She shrugged and turned to start walking away, and that's when I real-ized: She's not the one acting all odd today, I am! She's just wearing a slightly small T-shirt, and here I am, so distracted by her anatomy, I am totally losing track of who she is — my buddy. Nothing more, nothing less.

What a relief. She'd come clear across the cafeteria to rag on me some more, just a totally normal day. And she was waiting for my comeback, I could tell, she was turning away so slowly.

"It was the part about stapling it to my head that got me," I said.

She whirled back around and we smiled at each other. Like, *Oh, yeah, you. I know you!* "Yeah, well," she said.

I held my hand out to her and asked, "Truce?" It's what we used to say to each other after fistfights in our yards, when we were little and both sore losers. We'd smack each other around pretty good until one or the other of us was too tired or, occasionally, hurt, to fight anymore, and then the other would hold out a hand and say, "Truce?" It meant we wouldn't tell our parents, we wouldn't be a crybaby, that whatever was between us would stay right there between us, and we'd get on with the next game.

She shook my hand and, just like when we were younger, said, "Truce."

I watched the girls walk away, leave the cafeteria to

go out to the playground; I watched Zoe walk away flanked by the whisperers, with those stupid pens holding a lump of hair to the back of her head, and just smiled.

"You look like the cat who ate the canary," said Lou.

I was in too good a mood to bust his chops over that, even — even the fact that Lou talks like somebody's grandmother seemed good, nice, wholesome. Recognizable. I chugged my ginger ale and let the bubbles fill my head.

"Looks like somebody's in love," Gideon said, tossing his lunch bag toward the garbage can, but missing by a mile.

"Yeah, Gideon," I said, crushing the ginger ale can in my hand. "Why don't you go to the ATM, withdraw all your money, and buy yourself a clue."

"Denial is more than just a river in Egypt," Lou threw in.

I laughed, but decided again to go easy. Poor Lou. Such a goon.

"Love," Gideon crooned. "Tommy's in love. Love, love, love."

Gideon I have less patience for. I actually enjoy any excuse to beat on him, to be honest. But instead of whapping another fist into his spongy midsection, I turned to roll my eyes at Jonas, who, I felt sure, would know the truth. He's pretty logical, and he's known me since before we were born. But he was giving me this pissed-off look, no smile. Still mad about Windmill Man, obviously.

I shoved him and got out of the bench. "Get over it."

But I wasn't angry, not really. My feet weren't grabbing my socks or anything, I noticed.

Gideon slapped the table. "Lover boy," he taunted. "Oh, lover boy!"

I spun around to give Gideon a look I hoped was like the one Zoe'd given me earlier, that fierce look, like, back off if you know what's good for you. Gideon flinched. It was a quick flinch, but I caught it, and it unclenched my fists. He was scared, that was enough. I shrugged it off and smiled at him, my biggest smile.

"What?" he asked nervously.

I can't explain how happy the shaky anxiety in his voice made me. It made me feel generous. Let them think I'm happy, or in love, or in a crush — or been made a fool of — it didn't matter to me. I knew the truth: Zoe's my buddy and Gideon is a wimp. Everything is the way it's always been. I turned away from them again.

Gideon got in front of me, blocking my way and making kissy noises. I held up my palm. "Mmm, lover boy!" he whispered.

I pushed my palm hard into his puckered face, smooshing his lips and nose. "In your dreams," I said.

Gideon rubbed his face and whined. Lou was banging his head on the table, laughing. What a bunch of rejects my friends are. I decided I am definitely better friends with Zoe than any of these goofballs, and who could blame me? At least she doesn't drool when she laughs.

I tossed my garbage into the pail — two points — and headed out for the playground. They weren't messing up my improved mood, just because they don't GET it. They think it has to be some complicated thing going on between me and Zoe.

On the way toward the playground, I found a heads-up penny and picked it up. *Where were you when I needed you this morning?* I thought, but then resolved to appreciate luck whenever it felt like coming my way. Decided, *OK, here's a sign my luck is turning.* I slipped the penny into my shoe and leaned into the door to go out to the playground. On my way through, squinting in the bright sunlight, I felt my pocket, fully expecting to find my key there, suddenly.

It wasn't.

I checked my other pocket. No.

Scanning the playground, I saw Zoe sitting with CJ, Morgan, and Olivia, in a tight circle under the chestnut tree, their heads all bent toward the center, whispering. Some of the guys from soccer were kicking a ball around. Dex Pogostin waved at me, waved me over, but I pretended not to see him. I hoped he wouldn't be mad — he's a starter and amazing; it would be awesome to play wing to his center this year — but right then I just wasn't really in the mood to play soccer.

I wandered out past the swings toward the chainlink fence, where the outcasts usually hang. Gabriela Shaw, in fact, was sitting against the fence reading a book. I didn't want to attract her attention or make her think I was looking for some company, which I wasn't — I was actually looking for some alone. So I hooked a left and sat down facing a bush, my back to everybody.

The penny fell into the grass when I took off my sneaker and shook it. I flipped the penny hand to hand for a minute, thinking about luck, wondering if you are supposed to wish on a heads-up penny like when you throw one into a fountain, or if you just get vaguely good luck and that's that. I plunked the penny back into the shoe and pulled at blades of grass for a while. My arm still looked good to me, shaved like that, though compared to the other, hairy arm, maybe it looked a little feminine. I don't want to be girly or anything. Oh, well, I decided. It'll grow back. It's not a tattoo.

The sun was beating down hard on my head. It felt good, like it was cooking out whatever was left of my earlier mental derangement. Hard to believe it was fall already, back to school, back into the swing of the school year, when it still felt like summer, like we should all be flopping around the swim club, grubby and hungry, tossing a ball back and forth and smelling the charcoal heating up. Zoe and I had escaped the sun one afternoon going on a barefoot treasure hunt, and made up this thing that one of the lifeguards was on to us, just really as an excuse to duck into shady prohibited areas. We ran into what I guess was a huge storage closet and we were leaning against this stack of lounge chairs. My heart was pounding, even though I was the one who made up the thing about that lifeguard following us, so I knew we weren't in real danger, but my body didn't remember, I guess, because all my nerves were in a state of massive alert, my heart pounding and my eyes open wide, my breath coming fast and Zoe's, too — her face was right near mine, and I could see she was into it, too, her long fingers splayed on the white plastic webbing, not moving except for her breath, in a rhythm with mine. That's when the tower of chairs toppled over, giving us one big heart attack to share. We booked out of there fast, and only later discovered the gash up her leg. She was proud of the scar the rest of the summer.

I took a quick look around the upper field, to see if anybody was stalking me — wouldn't put it past Gideon and Lou and maybe even Jonas to sneak up on me, if they spotted me up here alone in the loser section of the playground — but they were nowhere to be seen, and the girls were still in that tight circle down below, under the chestnut tree. Gabriela wasn't looking at me, either. She looked pretty lonely, her head bent over that paperback, though maybe she was just involved in the plot. She's a pretty independent person, strong, I guess. She just seems so goofy it's hard to get past that, but when she's not right on top of you with all her positive feedback and supportive good cheer, you can see there's something sort of admirable in her. Runs in the family, I guess, because Zoe is like that, too. Under it all, just a strong, solid person, the kind of person I'd like to be.

And maybe am. I mean, I'm not the one with nightmares. I don't have to be protected from anything. I can handle pretty much whatever comes my way, right? I made Zoe laugh, back there in the cafeteria.

I took the pen out of my back pocket, tried to twirl it in my fingers. I used to be able to do this thing, twirl it from my thumb over-under fingers to my pinkie and back again, but I am seriously losing coordination lately. I gave up after a minute and uncapped the pen.

Summer, I wrote on my palm, then read it over a few times. Summer. *Hot as the sun is today,* I thought, *summer is definitely gone.* So unfair. Winter takes like a year to get through, and summer — is there anything faster than summer?

In smaller letters, to squeeze it in to the left of *Summer*, I wrote, *fast as.*

What's fast as summer?

Hello, Tommy, are you back to thinking you're some kind of poet or something?

I laughed slightly out loud to myself at the idea of that. No way. That would be like Jonas still thinking he could grow up to be Superman. No, just doodling, just writing on my hand like Mom hates me to do. I doodled on the side of my sneaker, too, to prove it. I wrote, *The Bomb.*

I'm not sure one hundred percent what that means, but Dex Pogostin had it written on his sneaker last year, and I always liked it. Not that I wanted to be Dex Pogostin, or copy him, as cool as Dex seems. I crossed it out. I wrote *BANG* instead. Which meant whatever you want it to mean, and anybody who asks is a dork for asking.

The bell rang. My legs obeyed. As I headed down the hill, I saw all the kids moving toward the door, jamming up there where it got tight.

Fast as summer, goes lunch period.

Oh, how brilliant. I should tell my mother. She'd get me on CNN.

I recapped the pen and shoved it into my back pocket, picking up the pace because you don't want to be late to Mrs. Shepard's class. At the last minute, though, passing through the spongy-padded area where the swings are, I slowed down. I didn't want to go in that dark school, I wanted to be out in the bright heat. For a second, I considered cutting, heading back up to that bush in the far reaches of the school property.

Sometimes I wonder if I am not the strong one but the weird one instead. I sure hope not. I would hate to be the weird one. I slapped my cheeks hard and hurried to my locker.

eleven

Jonas was at the lockers when I got there, but he didn't say anything and neither did I. I grabbed my loose-leaf and flung my locker door shut. What did he want, an apology? It was just a joke. He has to learn to be less sensitive about the whole nightmare thing, or he's just going to get teased, and by people who'll do him a lot more damage than I ever would. At least Zoe knows how to take a joke; she doesn't get all sulky and hurt.

My lock rattled behind me as I hurried down the corridor to English/social studies. I was the first kid there, so I took out my assignment pad and copied down, in the center of the first blank page, *Fast as summer.* But I still couldn't think of what to put with it. I closed the pad and stuck it back inside my loose-leaf.

"Mr. Levit?"

It hit me before I lifted my eyes that I was here alone in the classroom with The Sadist. What was I thinking?

"What?" I asked Mrs. Shepard, sounding more scared than I'd intended to let her know I was.

"Please distribute these." She was sitting behind her massive desk, this little, solid woman, holding a stack of brown paper bags outstretched toward me, across the piles of books.

I stood up. As I took the paper bags, I saw that the red nail polish had chipped off parts of a few of her fingernails. I almost smiled at her, realizing for the first time that she must have a life beyond torturing seventh graders — maybe she worked in a garden somewhere, or built shelves, and the digging or sanding chipped her nail polish. Maybe she has a sailboat, or a husband — she must have a husband, right? It's Mrs., not Miss or Ms. — and they might go out to dinner and send each other the kind of anniversary cards that have the extra paper half-glued in, and then maybe go in the shower together. Maybe that's a totally obvious thing everybody knows married people do at night, and nobody but me would be the slightest bit thrown off by it. Come to think of it, Mom's nail polish was chipped this morning, too.

I took the bags and turned away from Mrs. Shepard

before any questions could slip out of my mouth. That'd be brilliant — ask the teacher if she showers with her husband. The best way to handle sadistic teachers, I have learned, is not to make any kind of impression on them at all. They tend to pick on their favorites and their most hateds, but leave the rest of the class alone. I intend to be in that middle group, unremarkable — and any comment on her chipped nail polish or showering habits would certainly catapult me right out of the anonymity of that comfort zone.

I placed one paper bag on each desk, quickly but not carelessly, left the extras neatly stacked on Mrs. Shepard's desk, and was halfway back to my seat by the time Gabriela Shaw and Ken Carpenter were coming through the classroom doorway. First time I ever beat Ken Carpenter to a class. He looked surprised to see me. I sunk down into my chair. Who cares what he thinks, the dweeb.

When Zoe came in, just before the bell, I tilted my head in her direction, a greeting if she caught it or a nothing if she didn't, a just-stretching-my-neck, not committing to anything. She didn't catch it. I stretched my neck to the other side, too, then tried the flipping-my-pen-over-and-under-fingers trick again, but my co-ordination still wasn't working. I picked up the pen off the floor and sunk down low in my seat.

After the bell rang, Mrs. Shepard moved to the front of her desk and waited there with the tip of her tongue pointing disappointedly at her upper lip. Everybody shut up. I sat straight in my chair and placed the pen in the pen groove at the top of my desk.

"Your homework over the weekend . . ."

I slumped down again. Homework on the weekend? No wonder everybody calls her The Sadist. Give us a break. People were groaning all around the room.

"Is there a problem?" Mrs. Shepard asked, and Lou, the poor innocent geek, took that as an actual question she might be searching for an answer to.

"Usually teachers give us the weekend off," he explained sincerely. "To recuperate." Lou sits diagonally in front of me, but I couldn't look at him. You gotta feel sorry for a guy like that. I tightened my stomach muscles, as if I were the one about to get nailed. Poor soft Lou. I bet he had no idea he was asking for it. The rest of us all waited.

"Well, Mr. Hochstetter," Mrs. Shepard said. "Welcome to the seventh grade."

I tried to hold in my smile. She got him. He set her up and she didn't disappoint. In spite of myself I have to admit I sort of like Mrs. Shepard.

"Your homework for this weekend," she said again, "is called Bring Yourself in a Sack."

I swear I almost burst out laughing. *Control yourself, Thomas,* I told myself in Dad's voice. I was in serious danger of a laughing attack. *Happy birthday, dear Mrs. Shepard* . . .

OK, that left me practically panting with the effort not to fall on the floor laughing. Bring Yourself in the Sack? It sounded half-kinky, half-pathetic. I couldn't even listen to what in the world we were supposed to do over the weekend, I had to concentrate so hard on not cracking up, and to make it worse, next to me I heard a weird snorkeling noise from Zoe, so I knew she was dying, too. That's the thing with me and Zoe — sometimes we can be in a room full of people, and something will happen, like, last year one time, Lou sneezed in science class, and it blew one of Olivia Pogostin's pigtails forward, and me and Zoe were the only ones who saw it or at least the only ones who thought it was hilarious, and we both got sent to the principal's office. Mrs. Johnson didn't know what to do with us, we were falling over ourselves so much, practically passing out from lack of air intake, as we tried to explain what was so absolutely hysterical about Lou sneezing at Olivia's hair. The principal finally just got us paper cups of water and told us to calm down, but even sitting there in the office drinking out of pointy-bottom paper cups, as soon as Zoe and I made eye contact we were spitting and choking all over again.

So I knew better than to look over at Zoe now. *Bring Yourself in the Sack.* We'd be right back in Mrs. Johnson's office, for sure.

Mrs. Shepard was onto another topic, I noticed when I got my breathing under control, something about partnering up and you have to interview each other, then write a newspaper-style article about your partner. "Get details," she was saying. "Significant events in your subject's life. Favorite foods. What nobody knows about the subject."

I picked up my pen and chewed on the end of it. It sounded like sort of a cool project, I had to admit. Sometimes I think maybe I'll be a journalist, an investigative reporter, tracking down leads, writing my articles at the last minute, just making my deadlines. That's how I do most of my homework, now. Good training.

"Be creative," Mrs. Shepard was saying. "Ask probing questions."

I tried to think of some probing questions to ask somebody.

"Is there a problem?" Mrs. Shepard asked. Everybody jolted up, found partners. I looked to my right, and Zoe was looking back at me. "So?" she asked.

"Sure," I said, thinking, *Find out what nobody knows about her.* Jonas would be easier; I know lots more about him than anybody else does. But I saw he was working with Gideon already, which was just as well. If he's not talking to me, fine. Why should it bother me, if he's going to act like a baby? That's his problem.

Zoe picked up her desk and turned it ninety degrees so it faced mine. I did the same. I think my desk must be heavier than hers. She shoved hers forward an extra few inches to collide it into mine, then opened her notebook, all without looking up at me. I wasn't sure if she was still trying not to crack up about the Yourself in the Sack project or what, but I was determined to act normal, not tense like this morning. I flipped my notebook open to the English section and waited, chewing on my pen, to see how she thought we should start.

Her hair was still pulled back in that funny way, with pens stuck through. I was enjoying that when she asked, "You want to go first?"

I said OK and stiffened my face into a caricature of a craggy reporter, like from a TV movie. "Hello. Name please?" I asked her gruffly.

She rolled her eyes. "Come on," she said quietly. I guess it wasn't that great an imitation.

I whispered, "If The Sadist is half as rough as you . . ."

She smiled.

"I'm not taking any more chances today," I said, meaning, again, truce.

She blinked a few times and whispered, "Zoe Grandon."

I started to write down her name, forming the letters carefully, neatly, into my notebook. Zoe Grandon, a name I know as well as I know my own, but had I ever written it down before? I must've, right? On a birthday invitation, or a note to pass her sometime last year. It felt weird, writing her name with her watching me, watching my fingers form the letters of her name. My face was heating up again.

Make a joke, I warned myself. Don't get all freaky again. "How much do you weigh?" I asked her, making a period after the final *n* in Grandon. The end, done writing her name. I wiped the sweat off my forehead into my hair.

"Shut up," she teased back.

"Just tryin' to get the inside scoop, ma'am," I explained in I don't know what kind of accent. My voice cracked in the middle. I cleared my throat, to cover it up.

"No comment," she answered.

Sensitive about her weight, I wrote down, and waited for her to throw her pen or something at me. But when I flicked my eyes up to catch her expression, she was sunk way low in her chair, her eyes closed. I almost said I was sorry, she seemed so sad, so uncharacteristically sad. Zoe and I never say sorry to each other. We're buddies — we just plan revenge.

"How about we take turns asking?" she suggested without opening her eyes.

Oh, I thought. She's just gathering forces for her comeback. She's just getting ready to zap me; I didn't hurt her feelings or any such nonsense. I am such a sap. I have to quit thinking she's as simple and fragile as other people, underestimating her. I should know better by now, obviously. "Fine," I dared her. "Ask me anything." This time, I knew, I'd be able to handle whatever she came up with. My right leg started to pump, but it was just the adrenaline, just my body psyching itself up for the challenge.

"Do you like anybody?" she asked.

OK, she got me. I swallowed hard and pressed both fists into my thumping leg. Do I like anybody? I reminded myself — it's Zoe! She's setting me up, there's a joke, a put-down hidden in there somewhere. Keep it light or she'll think you're as much of a straightforward dork as Jonas. Say something smirky.

"Almost everybody," I came up with, and congratulated myself. That was a good one, Zoe would have to admit. I grinned, waiting for her comeback.

"But do you *like* anybody?"

I looked down at her name on my paper and thought, *Yes.*

I wasn't playing anymore, wasn't a little kid, her buddy, muddy and grubby and looking for the next advantage out in the tree house. She knew it, obviously, and she was calling me on it. Waiting there, staring me down to see if I had the courage to admit what I guess has been clear to the entire school all day.

"Yes," I said.

"Who?" Zoe asked me, as if she didn't know.

I watched her write my name on her paper, and had to open my mouth to breathe. *Tommy Levit.* It looked good in her round letters, neat and open, the *m*'s like a row of hills. She had paused after the *t* of Levit, pen hovering, then wrote, *likes,* then paused again.

"Who?" she asked again.

Her name was in my mouth. I swallowed it and whispered, "My turn."

She drew a blank line next to the *likes* and whispered back, "OK."

So I asked her, "Do you like anyone?"

Silence first, and then her whisper: "Yes."

I closed my eyes. I wanted her to say my name so bad.

I watched Zoe's pen doodle in the space above that

blank line, and thought for a second I saw her write a *z*. She is ballsy enough to just do it, to write what is true right out on paper. *Tommy Levit likes Zoe Grandon.* I waited. The tip of her pen touched the white paper again.

I just would've whispered, "Yes."

I realized I'd been staring at her head when she lifted only her eyes and asked, "Who is it? For you? That you like?"

You. I breathed in and out a couple of times. Did she want me to admit it? Or was I supposed to keep it up, this new kind of teasing, quieter and more complex? I didn't want to blow it. I knew the wrong thing could.

"No comment," I answered her, catching up, catching on, almost using the funny accent again but then, not. *No comment*, to prolong it, to stay in this zone, alone, together, right in English class, each knowing what the other was thinking (*YOU*) and knowing suddenly that we've both known for a while now. I knew she knew, and I knew she knew I knew, and we were so knotted up knowing together, we were breathing in rhythm together again, like that time this summer. I licked my lips to keep them from forming the word. *You.*

"Who do *you* like?" I whispered. *You. Please say it. You.*

She whispered, "No comment also," and then asked, even quieter, "Is it . . ."

Yes, I wanted to scream. I licked my lips again. *You know it is.*

She whispered, "Anybody I know?"

I couldn't play it anymore. She has always been quicker than me, smarter. I didn't trust myself to say anything but *you,* so I didn't say anything. I just let it hang there between us, hovering above our desks, and she did, too.

Her mouth opened and I saw her bottom teeth. A sound happened inside my throat, nothing I'd ever heard from myself before. It was like the squeak a balloon makes if you pinch its neck and release air very slowly.

She looked down, away from me, but a similar noise came from her. I couldn't stop staring at her. This girl I married at my fifth birthday party, my backdoor neighbor, my buddy, this girl I've seen practically every day of my life, and I couldn't get enough of looking at her forehead.

Until she looked up at me again. Why did I never see how blue her eyes were before, how many different colors of blue overlap there? Oh, man, did anybody ever feel this throttled and thrilled at once before? I was holding on to the sides of my desk so tight, I realized, my fingers were all cramped. I tried to let go, but couldn't.

"Zoe," I said. It was happening so fast, this new, this whole new amazing, overwhelming, between-us thing. *Fast as summer,* I thought.

Before her name was all the way out of my mouth, she asked me my favorite food.

My favorite food?

It released me, like the lights coming on at the end of a really intense movie, and you blink and remember where you are, quickly wipe away your tears, and shut your gaping mouth.

I said something stupid like "pineapple upside-down cake," which Nana was planning to make this weekend for Mom and Dad's party, so it was in some corner of my mind.

Food?

I tried to think of a question like that to ask her back, but I couldn't. I just slid down in my chair and watched her doodle over that blank next to my name, in the space where her name belonged, then fold the paper and place it at the corner of her desk, where my desk touched hers.

The top half of the note opened slowly, pulled away from the bottom half. When it stopped moving, I reached over, across my desk to the corner of hers, and covered the square of paper with my hand. I waited.

She didn't look up.

I pulled the paper onto my own desk and dropped my hands quickly into my lap. She still wasn't looking, so I tipped the note, which toppled and faced its open side toward Zoe. I swept it into my lap then, and, watching her not watching me, I unfolded it. My name in her rounded writing, next to the line loaded with her dark inky doodles. I touched the smudges with my thumb, covered them, then lifted the paper up onto my desk again. Zoe was doodling in her notebook, not with me anymore.

I shielded the note in the curve of my arm and drew a new line in the space underneath what she'd crossed out. In the blank, I wrote her name for the second time. Zoe Grandon.

Tommy Levit likes Zoe Grandon.

I folded the paper again, along the creases she had already made.

twelve

a momentary panic kept me from dropping the note on her desk when the bell rang, so I sat back down and wrote, *For Zoe Only* on the outside. I'm daring, but not that much. I stood beside her desk for a second or two, in the clatter of everybody else gathering up their stuff and rushing out, but she was still writing her newspaper feature about me. I tilted my head to try to read what she'd written there, and saw my little cousin Zachary's name. She wrote about Zachary? I glanced to the front but Mrs. Shepard wasn't paying attention so I peeked again. "Tommy is very proud of what a good older cousin he is to Zachary. He taught the four-year-old the name of every dinosaur this summer, and

Tommy himself doesn't even care about dinosaurs, which means he had to learn all those facts himself first, which just shows what kind of person he is."

I laid the note on her desk and left when I saw she had covered it protectively with her hand.

I didn't think she was even paying attention when I was telling about Zachary and the dinosaurs at the pizza place after we all bought school supplies the day before yesterday. And she's right, I don't really care that much about dinosaurs, and it is important to me to be a good big cousin. I hadn't written anything so true and revealing about her for my article; it was hard to concentrate on it, with the note, the most important note of my life, clutched in my other hand. I just wrote a bunch of nonsense, how she's a good sport in every meaning — athletic and up for anything, always in a good mood, easy to be with. I wrote that she's faster and she's got a better arm than most boys her age, and that she doesn't care about how she looks or jewelry or stuff like most girls her age. It wasn't much of an article. I don't think *The New York Times* will want to publish it or anything, plus there were probably a thousand spelling mistakes. But the conclusion was OK, I think. "In conclusion, Zoe Grandon is everything you could want in a friend — and more."

I liked that when I came up with it because I figure Mrs. Shepard will think I mean she has even more of what you want in a friend than you could ever hope for, but what I really meant was that she is everything you would want in a friend and also in a more-than-a-friend.

I waited right outside the classroom door. We have gym last, and I thought maybe we'd walk down the hall to the gym together, not talking, just being together, knowing. And then, I decided, before she pushes open the door to the girls' locker room, I could ask her, quietly so just she can hear, "Will you go out with me?" and she would say yes, and then we'd go to the locker rooms and change, get ourselves under control. She'd probably tell her friends in there, but that would be OK with me. The guys would find out later and ask me about it, and I'd just shrug and say, yeah, and if Jonas wants to act all superior like he knew all along I was in love with Zoe, then fine, let him. I could afford to be generous today.

She was unfolding the note when I spied back into the classroom, craning my neck around the corner. I pulled my head back into the hall quickly and rested it against the concrete wall with my eyes closed.

CJ and Morgan crowded the doorway. "Come on, Zoe," CJ pleaded.

"Yeah, come on," added Morgan.

Zoe stepped through the doorway, with her head bent down. I was staring at her, waiting for her to look at me that way again, and then we'd walk down the hall silently together like I'd planned. Instead, CJ grabbed her and whispered something that ended with "... anything?"

Zoe shrugged. She went with CJ down the hall, away from me.

"What's wrong?" Jonas asked me.

"What's wrong with you?" I screamed. His eyes opened wide and he backed two steps away.

"I'll tell you what's wrong with him," I heard Gideon say from inside the classroom.

Jonas and I both tilted our heads to look back in. Gideon was standing beside Mrs. Shepard's desk, holding his paper up like it was a work of art for us to admire. We were too far away to see what Gideon was all flushed and acting the fool over, so Jonas and I stepped back through the doorway. It's weird; even though we're twins, we are SO not identical, but sometimes when Jonas moves or stops moving, my body is doing the exact same thing at the exact same time, so it feels like, in my peripheral vision, I'm catching a reflection of myself, only sweeter-looking, softer. That's how it was stepping back into the classroom — our right feet swung forward, but our bodies hadn't moved over them yet, and then our shoulders pulled back, away from Gideon and his paper. And we froze.

"JONAS LEVIT IS TERRIFIED DREAMER" it said on top, in capital letters. I grabbed the paper out of Gideon's hand and read the beginning: "Jonas Levit is nearly thirteen years old, but he is terrified of the full moon. He has nightmares of a windmill chasing him, trying to kill him. Jonas seems like a nice normal boy, singing in the chorus and laughing along with his friends, but underneath he is a total wuss."

That's as far as I got, with Jonas reading it over my shoulder, and Gideon grinning in front of me, before I crumpled his paper as tight as I could.

"Hey!" Gideon yelled, grabbing my fists.

"I'm not terrified of the full moon," Jonas said calmly.

"You are such a dead man," I growled at Gideon.

"*You* are!" Gideon yelled back. His cheeks were blotchy red and his grip on my fists was tight. "Give that back!"

Mrs. Shepard came out from behind her desk and tapped the toe of her high-heeled shoe. We all turned and looked at her. She was waiting with her arm outstretched.

"He crumpled up my paper," Gideon whined.

"He crumpled up my paper," I imitated.

"Enough," said Mrs. Shepard.

I tightened my clutch on the trash he'd written about my brother, then thrust it toward the teacher. Fine. But he'd pay. I stormed out of the classroom.

Jonas was gone.

I wasn't sure whether to go straight to the lockers and find Jonas, see if he was OK, ask if he wanted me to beat up Gideon for him or what, or wait and make sure Gideon knew he'd gone too far. I decided to wait for Gideon. I'd way rather threaten than apologize.

I stood outside the classroom and listened to the whine of his voice complaining to Mrs. Shepard that I had grabbed his paper, he'd just been doing what she said, writing what nobody ever knew about his subject, now the pen was all smeared and how would she be able to read his masterpiece. *Waaa, waaa, waaa.* My hands were tight fists.

Mrs. Shepard finally responded by saying something about he was going to be late for his next class. So out he lumbered, this saggy hulk of a guy who thinks he's so great because once he shaved and now he wrote an exposé of a kid who never did anything mean to anybody.

I grabbed him by the collar and yanked hard,

pulling him down the hall away from the classroom. "Let's go, Weld. You really asked for it this time."

"We're gonna be late for gym," he said, and the bell rang in agreement.

"No, we're not," I said. I let go of his stupid shirt. "I'm not going to beat the crap out of you now. I'm gonna make you wait."

"Oh, I'm so scared." He slammed into the locker room door.

I caught it right behind him and said, "You should be."

I changed into my gym suit fast, not talking to anyone. I wanted to make up the time I'd wasted, get out there into the gym and find Zoe, not let too much time pass, and beat Gideon out there also, so he couldn't ambush me.

I yanked off my high-tops to get out of my normal shorts, but realized as I was pulling on my gym shorts that I should be careful not to lose my lucky penny. I banged one sneaker and then the other against the bench, but nothing, not one coin, fell out. The bell rang. I stomped into my sneakers and tied them tight. I think you still get the luck — it's finding the penny that brings the luck, right? *Find a penny, pick it up, and all the day you'll have good luck.* There's nothing about *and you'd better not lose it.* That's not a rule, the thing with sticking it in your sneaker, that's just my own superstition. I double-bowed the laces as quickly as I could and pushed myself out of the locker room, assuring myself, *It's OK, it's OK.*

In the high-ceiling echoes of the gym, I squeaked around in my tight sneakers, searching for her, but even after Mr. Brock blew his whistle, Zoe didn't show.

Next thing I knew, I was facedown on the shiny wood floor, staring at the red paint of the foul line, with all hundred fifty pounds of Gideon Weld on my back. As much as I flailed around and tried to get the advantage, there was nothing I could do; he was sitting on me, punching me between the shoulder blades and complaining that I had smudged his masterpiece. I tried to yell back that he had no right to write those things about Jonas, but I could barely breathe, never mind argue. I tried to concentrate on sucking in some air. Gideon's feet were plunked beside my face, and as I lay there suffocating, I realized, *I am getting beaten up by a kid who wears beige socks to gym. Can I be any more pathetic?*

Mr. Brock yanked Gideon off me and sent him, sobbing, to the principal's office. Half the gym class was surrounding me, checking me out, the girls all sympathetic and the boys, most of them, I bet, thinking what a wimp I was, getting the stuffing beat out of me by Gideon Weld. I shrugged them all off, scanning again for Zoe, who still wasn't there.

She at least would've gotten a laugh out of it, Gideon in his beige socks, pummeling me. I wiggled my shoulders around, trying to loosen up the charley horse the big lug had given me. I tried to feel vindicated that he was the one who'd be curled up in a chair alone in the carpeted air-conditioning of the main office instead of me, and tried to feel smart, thinking he'd get his now, he'd be suspended or at least have his mother called, while I had Carla Obaseki sitting down next to me, asking was I OK and what was wrong with that weird guy, anyway?

I just shrugged at her, barely even glanced at her body. I didn't feel vindicated or smart, not at all. "He's not weird," I told Carla, and went to the water fountain.

I took a few long sips of the metallic water, but it wasn't helping. Mr. Brock blew his whistle. I didn't care. I wanted Gideon back in here, or me and him, out in the playground. I wanted to beat the living crap out of him, feel my fists hitting his jaw and his stomach, tearing through him. And even, here's the really weird part, I wanted him back in here pummeling me — for blurting out about Windmill Man, for setting Jonas up like I did, even for writing her name in the blank space of that note and handing it over to her, because if that was wrong, if that was the whole wrong way to handle it, I just succeeded in one day in turning my two best friends completely against me.

I hauled off and threw my right fist like a fastball straight into the cold, painted concrete wall, trying my hardest to shatter it. It was in my head to bring down the wall, the gym, the whole sorry school, right on top of myself.

Surprise, surprise. I didn't make a dent.

thirteen

I knew I should sit down in the seat next to Jonas. He had moved over toward the window when I climbed onto the bus, without acknowledging me exactly. He couldn't have known what happened with Gideon, I don't think, and even if he somehow had heard, I wasn't sure what he'd think — that I had been defending him, or just that Gideon had humiliated both Levit boys in one day. Either way, sitting next to him would be a way of declaring a truce, of saying, *Hey, we're on the same side.* Of saying sorry, I guess.

I sat in the seat across the aisle.

His curly head was bent over his notebook, already grinding away at his homework, on a Friday afternoon. He didn't say anything, not *hello*, not *how was gym*, not *you bastard, revealing what's private to Gideon Weld*. I watched him, wondering how angry he was and what he was planning to do to me in revenge. Maybe nothing. *A reasonable man*, Dad calls himself when he's angry at me, and I know he's really saying, *Why can't you be reasonable like me, like Jonas?* Jonas is going to be a reasonable man, you can just tell. What I'm going to be is totally up for grabs.

A sixth-grade boy paused beside me and started to turn, to sit. My hand shot out. "Taken," I blurted. He looked a little surprised but was smart enough not to argue. He tossed his book bag into the seat in the row behind me. I caught Jonas's head moving, but I couldn't be sure if he'd given me a dirty look because he was back to being bent over his notebook by the time I checked.

Fine. I looked out the window, squinting in the glare, and saw Zoe crossing the beige expanse of sidewalk, coming toward our bus. My forehead hit the windowpane. I shaded my eyes and watched her walk. Solid and sure, beside CJ, whose footsteps seemed weirdly mechanical.

Zoe.

I prayed I hadn't royally screwed everything up with her. If she sits down next to me, I bargained, it is all OK. We can walk down the street together after we get off the bus. Maybe I'll touch her hand with the outside of mine, brush the skin of her arm with my smooth arm skin, no hair in the way, and look into those blue eyes again, and maybe I won't even have to ask her out, she'll just know.

She was nodding at CJ Hurley by the wall, her head tilted forward as she listened. Her hair was down over her shoulders again. It was really shiny. Or maybe it was just the slanted sun on it.

Breathe, Levit. Breathe.

I grabbed my loose-leaf out of my backpack and yanked the assignment pad from inside it. Rummaged in the front pocket for a pen, uncapped it with my teeth, and found the right page. *Fast as summer.*

I glanced out the window. Zoe was heading for the bus. I had to write fast.

> *I could fall in love with you*
> *Fast as summer*
> *Could you fall in love with me?*

I tore out the page, folded the paper, bit it in my teeth while I dropped the pad and pen into my backpack's main compartment, and kicked it under the seat in front of me. I jammed the note into my front left pocket and kept staring out the window, feeling Zoe moving up the aisle toward me, praying she'd sit in the empty space beside me.

I touched the note in my pocket. It crinkled. Maybe I'd hand it to her after Jonas went over the fence to our yard, and I could stand with Zoe on her grass, and watch her read it.

She sat down beside me.

Good. *You're the man,* I told myself. I tried to hold in the smile.

I could feel heat coming off her with my skin. Outside the window, trees were whipping past us as we picked up speed out the exit of school, paused at the stop sign, then lurched onto the road. I cooled my hot cheek against the window. We rode by the big sign my mom had helped raise money for:

BOGGS, MASSACHUSETTS
Village of Sidewalks

I tried to think of something funny to say to Zoe about the sign. *Quite a claim to fame, huh?* No, that's terrible. *Pretty exciting place we live, huh?* Anything I came up with sounded depressingly like something Lou would say. So instead I just sat there next to her. I gave myself a deadline of the first stop to come up with an opening — if not a witty remark about the BOGGS sign, at least a something, a start of a conversation.

How had I started in Mrs. Shepard's? Something went right, in there; I should come up with something similar here, to get rolling again. Oh, yeah. *Name, please.*

OK, no way that's going to work twice. Be funny, be smart, say something that will make her smile.

We got there fast. I was still trying to think.

"You cut gym," I said, with a minimum of wit, but we were pulling away from the curb again. It was my deadline.

She answered, "Do you like CJ?"

What? Do I like CJ? Hurley? Why would she begin to think that? All I'd said was "you cut gym." She wouldn't meet my eyes with hers. She lifted her knees so they were braced against the seat in front of us and started fiddling with her shoelace.

Either she didn't read my note after all, or she didn't get what I was saying in it, or she read it and got it but was choosing to ignore it.

OK, then, one at a time: I saw her reading it, so that's out. There wasn't a huge amount of ambiguity; I wrote it flat out there: *Tommy Levit likes Zoe Grandon.* So there's no way she didn't get it. Which meant she was choosing to ignore it. Which left me with two choices: ignore it, too, pretend I never handed her that note, pretend what had happened between us today, or I guess what I thought happened between us, but maybe she didn't think happened at all, maybe I was completely off base and deluded — pretend none of that happened; or the stupid, humiliating, put-yourself-out-there-into-never-return-from-be-a-fool-land choice.

Which, of course, I chose.

Don't, I was screaming silently at myself. *Don't make it worse.* But I asked her, "Did you read my note?" My voice sounded shaky and weak.

She didn't answer.

"Oh," I said after a while.

The bus wobbled forward and around the corner. I let my shoulder hit hers. She moved away.

Well, I was just kidding, anyway. She wouldn't be stupid enough to think I really meant I liked her, would she?

I shoved the second note, my stupid, nonrhyming *faster than summer* poem note, farther into my pocket, the left one, the one without a hole so there'd be no chance of this thing, for one, getting away from me today. In case anybody would foolishly think I was be-ing something other than just a wise guy.

You know I was kidding, right? In that note?

The sides of my mouth weren't cooperating. No grin would come, no sarcastic comment. OK, then, plan B: Grab her, shake her, pound a fist through her teeth. Snap that bra strap so hard it zings her into tomorrow, makes her cry.

Don't cry yet, I begged myself.

Across the aisle, Jonas yelled, "Zoe!"

We both looked over at him. Was sweet, soft Jonas going to try and save me again? Rescue me, like I was some pathetic little kid, scared and in need of protection? Jonas, who still cries easily and has nightmares and can't defend himself?

Go for it, Jonas, I prayed. *Please.*

"We're going bowling tonight," he told Zoe.

It took me a second to figure out what in the world he was talking about. We were going bowling? Nobody said anything to me about going bowling. But wait — actually that did sound familiar. What was Dad saying this morning as we were leaving, about bowling? That maybe we'd go bowling tonight to celebrate something. Their anniversary? But they don't so much love bowling, they think it's too noisy and that Jonas and I get too competitive — oh, yeah. The a cappella thing, the chorus Jonas had tried out for over the summer, and if he found out he didn't make it . . .

Oh, man. I'd forgotten all about it. I am such a lousy brother.

So he didn't make it. I'd been half-hoping he wouldn't; I wasn't sure I could stomach all the celebrations of how gifted my brother was, and then have to get dragged around to his concerts and rehearsals and performances, thank my grandmother for remembering to get me a booby-prize present, so I wouldn't feel bad when she brings him his gift to each triumphant production. She never forgets to bring a little something for the superstar's brother, gotta hand it to Nana.

But the truth was, I didn't feel happy, or even relieved. Poor Jonas. He really wanted this. He didn't talk for two days before his audition, to save his voice, and it honestly is a beautiful voice. I kind of like to listen to him sing myself.

Those jerks, I thought. Bunch of croonier-than-thou losers. They don't deserve him. Of course, the fact that I had totally forgotten about it made me that much more willing to beat somebody up for him, to make him think I'm not as much of a turd as I actually am.

"Bowling?" Zoe asked him.

"Yeah."

He met my eyes; I shook my head. I hadn't told Zoe

about his audition, I hadn't told anybody, because he's a pretty private person. I don't know if it was more he didn't want to jinx it or didn't want to show off that he got an audition or didn't want to have everybody know about it if he got rejected, but anyway he asked me not to say anything, and for once I was a decent friend and brother and kept my mouth shut. *See?* I thought. *I'm not a complete lowlife.*

An incomplete lowlife. Great. Congratulations.

"So, you want to come?" Jonas asked Zoe.

I watched her and waited, not knowing which way I was rooting. If she says no, it's over and at least I don't have to face her until Monday. If she says yes, it means the whole night together, a whole evening of feeling tense and trying not to blurt out my feelings all over the place. *Our worst nightmare,* Zoe and I had joked over the summer — *is a feelings conversation. Why are people always trying to tell each other their feelings? Ick.* We were having a catch out in the parking lot of the swim club. We'd promised to shoot each other if we ever tried to have a feelings conversation.

Oops. What did I think I was blurting out in that ridiculous note, if not my feelings? Her worst nightmare, served up by me, thank you very much. No wonder she was acting all cold toward me. She was supposed to be shooting me, after all; and here she was, shooting me down.

But maybe there's still a chance, I thought. Maybe I misunderstood, when she asked if I liked CJ. Maybe that wasn't her trying to fix me up with CJ at all — maybe she just had a funny story to tell about CJ and was wondering if I was friends with her, or maybe it was back to the comment about CJ's bun and she wanted to tell me why in the world she'd had a bun herself today, with pens in it. And we'd get past the note, we'd pretend it never happened, and we'd laugh together, about whatever she wanted. Everything would be normal again. If she said she'd come bowling.

"I can't," she answered. Answered both of us.

"Oh," said Jonas.

I stared out the window and silently thanked my brother for his attempt. *You win some, you lose a lot,* Dad says.

Next to me, Zoe said, "Um."

I wasn't lifting my forehead off the windowpane. I closed my eyes and we were back in class, breathing in rhythm together. Her pen writing my name.

"Because," she whispered.

I held my breath. *Yes? Because?*

"If you want to ask out CJ," Zoe whispered to me, "you should."

I opened my eyes. The trees and houses were flying by, backward. I tried to think of something devastating to say to Zoe. *Yeah, just what I want to do, ask out CJ. I always write down that I like somebody when I want to ask out somebody else.* I rubbed my swollen knuckles from when I'd punched the gym wall and wished I'd broken my whole hand and gotten taken by ambulance to the hospital, so I wouldn't be sitting here on the bus, trapped in this seat next to Zoe-friggin'-Grandon, who got so grossed out when I said I liked her that she cut gym to find me a booby-prize decoy to like instead.

I stomped my feet on the bus floor to unclench them.

Zoe stood up and walked away from me, up to the front of the bus.

I slammed my head into the window and tightened my eyes to hold in the tears. *Not here,* I told myself. *Not now.*

You're the man, I told myself. But I knew it wasn't true.

fourteen

Zoe was waiting in the well of steps before the bus stopped, with Mrs. Horvath complaining that you have to wait behind the white line until the bus is completely stopped, but Zoe didn't care. Mrs. Horvath sighed, cranked open the door, and released Zoe, who sprinted toward home.

Jonas and I followed her off. When the bus had made the turn up the street, I said to Jonas, "So you didn't get it? The chorus thing?"

He shook his head sadly.

"Stupid-heads." I kicked a rock. "Bunch of armpits."

Jonas made an attempt at a snicker, but it wasn't completely genuine. He usually likes it when I get creative with insults.

"Want me to beat them all up for you?" I offered.

"Yeah," he said. "Like you did with Gideon?"

I pushed him. "What do you mean?"

"I heard you sure showed him in gym class, giving him the old back maneuver."

I opened my mouth to protest, but he was smiling at me, so I shrugged instead. "Yeah, well, he deserved it. I hope his fists are good and sore."

"Good to know I have you protecting me," Jonas mocked.

"Somebody has to," I mumbled. We were crossing Zoe's lawn, and I didn't want to watch her, fumbling with her keys at her back door. We were going to have to pass right beside her. I slowed down to give her a chance to get in before we reached her.

"Nobody has to protect me," Jonas said.

"When you ask for it, saying stuff about the full moon . . . ?"

"I thought you agreed with Gideon about that," Jonas whispered.

"I do."

"So . . . ?"

Zoe was still at her back door. If we walked any slower, we'd be standing still.

"So why don't you stand up for yourself?" I asked Jonas. "You let him get away with it, you just, like, ask for humiliation. Tell him he's an idiot. Punch him in the mouth."

"Maybe he's right." Jonas shrugged. "What do I know about the moon? And the facts of the moon aren't about to change just because one kid bloodies up another kid."

I breathed in the smell of grass; someone must've mowed Zoe's lawn today. Sometimes I think Jonas is way smarter than I am. Sometimes I wish I could be him instead of me. If I had just waited and let him get out into the world before me, instead of rushing to be born first, maybe we would be each other and I wouldn't have to be Tommy. He'd be the one who passed the note.

As we got near Zoe, Jonas called over to her, "See you tomorrow maybe?"

She dropped her keys.

Jonas raised his eyebrows at me, twice, and then asked, "You guys hitting tennis balls all day again tomorrow?"

Zoe stood up and jingled her keys in her palm, while her eyes rose slowly to meet mine. *Sorry*, I could see her thinking.

"No," I said, and bolted for home. I didn't think I could face either of them right then. I waited for Jonas to unlock the door for me. I didn't talk to him, blew off the plate of cookies Mom had left out for us. I went upstairs, took the phone off the charger, and brought it with me into the bathroom, where I leaned my elbows on the window ledge and watched the window of Zoe's room until I saw her.

I ducked so she wouldn't see me if she looked out. She was pulling her tight, little brown T-shirt, the root of all evil, over her head. She pulls off her shirts the cool way, the way the lifeguards at the swim club do it — elbows up overhead, grabbing the back, rather than arms crossed in front and grabbing the bottom, the way I do it when I forget. I didn't see much of anything — that's not why I was looking, anyway. I just saw her elbows in the air and the T-shirt passing her belt loops before she walked away from the window. I stayed there, crouched, watching her empty room. When she crossed back in front of the mirror, she was wearing her favorite sweatshirt, the one she calls Big Blue. It's as soft as my mother's satin pillowcases. One time this past summer, I had wanted her to lend it to me when she soaked me with the hose, but she refused. *Nobody touches Big Blue*, she said, so, of course, I had to chase her all over her yard, grabbing at it. I didn't get the sweatshirt, but I tackled her pretty good, knocked her to the wet grass, so she was as wet and filthy as I was by the time we got called in for bed. I guess we were flirting. That's the night Mom made a whole thing of it. *What are you doing, rolling around on the grass with Zoe? What's going on here? You can tell me!*

When I told her "NOTHING!" I thought I was telling the truth, but maybe Mom knew better than I did what I was doing. She watched me avoiding her attempts at eye contact, stomping up the stairs to get out of my wet clothes and be alone in my room, and said something, like, *OK, if you say so.* I yelled down the stairs that she had no idea what she was talking about, that Zoe and I were just fighting.

Maybe I secretly knew we were flirting. Maybe I've known for a while that I've been feeling (oh, no — that dreaded word) different about Zoe than just buddies, but was smart enough until today to keep it to myself.

Zoe was either lying down on her bed or had left her room. She clearly wasn't coming back to stare out her window in hopes I'd be kneeling here in my bathroom, watching, waiting, like some lunatic pervert lovesick wacko.

I dialed information and got CJ Hurley's phone number.

I sat on the closed toilet seat with my head between my knees and the phone in both hands on top of my head for a while. CJ is cute, I guess. I bet a lot ·of people would think she's even cuter than Zoe, and girlier, absolutely girlier. If you're going to bother dealing with girls at all, with having a girlfriend in the first place, she may as well be a really girly one. Otherwise why not just hang out with the guys? As stupid and annoying as the guys can be, at least they don't make you feel all inside-out. And anyway, CJ is special, a dancer, somebody I've always admired. She seems like a nice enough person, though nervous, but that's OK; people are nervous sometimes. You shouldn't hold it against them. So what if she can't throw a ball or crack a joke? That's not the most important thing. A girlfriend is just, you know, you have one. It's sort of something you do. Maybe I've made too big a deal of it. You don't have to be best friends with a person to go out with her. In fact it's probably a whole lot better if you aren't. Less complicated. It's too complicated being friends with a girl in the first place. When you're six, it's one thing. By seventh grade, it's time to just go out with them or avoid them. *That will be my plan from now on,* I decided.

I guess she must like me, if she told Zoe to ask me to ask her out. So CJ wants me to ask her out. Good. It's better to be wanted than to want. Way better. That way you're in control.

I dialed CJ's number and waited through a few rings.

"Hello?"

"Hello," I said. "CJ there?"

"This is CJ," she said.

"Oh. It's Tommy," I said. "Levit."

"Hi," she whispered.

"So." I took a deep breath and considered asking how she was or saying something about her hair, but decided instead to just get to the point. "You want to go out with me?"

"OK," she answered.

"OK," I repeated. "Great."

She didn't say anything.

"CJ?"

"Yes?"

"Oh. I just . . . Did you tell Zoe to tell me to ask you out?"

Nothing, then, "Um . . ."

"Never mind," I said quickly.

"Did, if, did she, um, say . . ."

"I gotta go," I told her, my new girlfriend. I hung up before she could say good-bye or anything else and put my head back down between my knees.

fifteen

I handed over my high-tops in trade for the multicolored, smooth-soled bowling shoes with ratty, knotted laces, and tried not to think whose grubby feet had sweated in them last. Jonas was already over at our lane, tying his, while Mom and Dad stood at the counter discussing whether to pay for two rounds up front or try one and see if we were all still in the mood or too hungry. I thought of saying we could just get hot dogs and keep playing if we were hungry, but I decided to try out keeping a thought to myself and went over to Jonas instead.

He was watching the empty bowling lane stretched out in front of us, his forearms resting on his knees.

"I'm gonna slaughter you," I tried, sitting beside him on the hard orange plastic bench.

"Probably," he said.

"Would you stop it?" I hit him with my bowling shoe. "You are so incredibly depressing."

"Just honest," he said, but smiled. "Maybe depressing and honest."

I put my bowling shoes on. He watched me.

"The chorus thing?" I asked.

"My own fault," he mumbled. "I had no right, counting on it. What are the chances you make something like that? Winning the lottery, you know? No right to be discouraged, you don't win the lottery."

"You pay your money, you take your shot," I said, quoting our father.

"But yeah," he whispered.

"Discouraged," I repeated. "What would be the opposite of that? Couraged? Courageous?"

"Encouraged?" Jonas suggested.

"Oh, yeah," I said.

He laughed. I finished tying my shoes. We looked around to find Mom and Dad; they were at the snack bar, being handed a jumbo box of popcorn.

"They feel bad for you," I told Jonas.

"Talk about depressing. If they keep cheering me up, I'm going to need Prozac by Sunday."

"They really, well, we all thought you'd make it. You deserved to."

"The bastards," he said.

"The bastards," I agreed.

"Thanks." He spread his arms along the back of the bench and asked, "Do you like her?"

"Who?" I asked, glancing back at our parents, who were loading large sodas onto a plastic tray. "Mom? She's OK. A little too nosy, but she means well."

He gave me a look. "Zoe."

"Oh." For one microsecond I considered telling Jonas what had happened. "Oh, yeah," I said sarcastically, double-bowing my shoelaces and regaining my senses. "I love a girl who'll humiliate me in front of the whole school. That really turns me on."

"Today I just got this feeling . . ."

I clutched my throat like I was choking at the mention of that word.

"OK, OK, but I did."

Mom and Dad were heading toward us.

"No," I said. "Zoe?" My voice cracked on her name. I turned away from Jonas and kicked the bench. "No way. Anyway, I asked out CJ."

"Hurley?" The look of surprise on my brother's face was priceless.

"You know any other CJs?"

"No."

"So," I said.

"Really?" he asked, his eyes round and huge as the bowling balls ejecting from the machine, rolling into place for our game. "When?"

"This afternoon. I called her."

He blinked, finally. "And?"

"Yeah."

"Wow." He shook his head. "So it's, you're, a done deal?"

I didn't answer.

"Were you scared?" he asked.

I scrunched up my face and shrugged. "Of what?"

"I'd be scared," Jonas said solemnly. "Forget an audition. That would be truly terrifying."

"What would be?" Mom asked, leaning over the bench.

"Asking out a girl," Jonas answered.

"Who's asking out a girl?" Mom squealed. "Jonas, is there a girl you like now, too?"

"Too?" I asked, but meanwhile Jonas was saying, "No, Tommy."

"You asked Zoe out?" Mom asked me.

What, does the entire world see right through my skull into my personal thoughts?

"No," Jonas exclaimed.

Dad was setting the overloaded tray down on the table behind the bench, trying not to spill, with his glasses slipping down his nose.

"Tommy asked a girl out!" Mom announced to him and anyone within the county limits who might or might not be interested.

I sunk down and tried to meld with the orange plastic bench.

"Zoe?" Dad guessed, and tipped over a soda. He grabbed a wad of napkins from a dispenser and cursed; then, while sopping up the sticky mess, asked me, "What did she say?"

"CJ!" I yelled.

"She said what?" Dad asked. "Zoe said 'CJ'? Is that an expression? What does that mean?"

That means she doesn't like me, I thought, but answered, "I asked out CJ Hurley. A girl in our grade."

"Oh," Dad said, and turned to Mom. "I thought you said he liked Zoe."

Mom shrugged dramatically. "I thought he did, the way he's been carrying on, but what do I know? Is CJ that cute little ballerina?"

Jonas nodded.

"Oh, she's adorable," Mom enthused, and rushed around the bench to squeeze in next to me. "So, did she say yes? How did you ask her? Tell me the whole thing! This is so exciting! Were you nervous?"

"No," I said. "Are we bowling at all tonight?"

Jonas went to the desk and wrote our names on the score sheet, so they appeared large and lit, overhead. Meanwhile Dad was massaging Mom's shoulders, saying, "Boy, I remember being so nervous the first time I asked your mother out, my right knee was shaking."

I looked up at him in shock. I'd never heard that part of the story before. "Really?" I asked. *Your right knee?* I was thinking. *Maybe it's genetic, a right knee tremor brought on by liking a girl.*

"He kicked me," Mom said.

He gave her shoulders a visible squeeze and let go. "I did not, you brat."

"Almost."

"Tommy, you're up first," Jonas called back to me.

I walked slippingly up to the ball return, wanting to hear more about Dad's freaking-out knee. I didn't want them to think I was interested or anything, though, so I chose a ball and whipped it as hard as I could down the lane. It was heading straight down the middle and I thought, *Well, good, I deserve a strike, I deserve to bowl a perfect game tonight.*

In the last stretch, though, it curved slightly to the left, and by the time it reached the pins, it was almost in the gutter. One pin fell. The one next to it wobbled, considering it, and reluctantly lay down. Like it was doing me this huge favor. I turned back to the ball return for my second attempt and bowled a gutter ball almost from the start.

"Good try," said Dad when I thudded onto the bench beside him, while Jonas took his turn.

"It's the attempt that matters," I quoted.

Dad hit me lightly upside the head. "This was a tough day for your brother," he said quietly.

"I know."

"It's very hard to put yourself out there, audition for something you want really badly and are unlikely to get."

I grunted and checked out the ceiling. Just what I needed was a lecture.

Jonas bowled a spare and came to sit beside me, flushed with happiness, while Mom took her turn.

"Great job," Dad said to him.

Jonas shrugged modestly, but his cheeks were still bright red, like whenever he's psyched. He can't hide what he's feeling at all.

"I was just telling Tommy," Dad said to Jonas. "About when I interviewed for my first job out of college."

"You were?" I asked. Sometimes it's impossible not to bust his chops.

"I was about to, when I was interrupted by Jonas's bowling prowess."

I groaned. Jonas's cheeks calmed down. Too much praise can really make a person feel like a loser. Like you look like you need bucking up so desperately.

"Your turn," Mom told Dad. She'd gotten four or five down, beating me. I propped my elbows on my knees and rested my head in my hands.

Dad held up his palm. "It'll hold a sec."

Mom raised her eyebrows and leaned against the desk chair expectantly.

"I was just saying to the boys here an important thing about life."

Mom sunk down into the chair and made a show of checking her watch. She's a chop-buster, too.

"When I went on my first interview," Dad said, looking up toward the fluorescent lights. "Oh, I was so impressed with myself. I talked to the woman interviewing me about the philosophy I'd studied, my beliefs — I thought she was going to put me in charge of the entire school system."

"Did you get the job?" Jonas asked reluctantly. We'd heard this story before, but Dad so enjoyed telling it, and interrupting would just prolong the agony.

"She tossed me out on my butt," he said.

We laughed. He'd never put it quite that way before.

Dad grinned at us. "Broke my heart. I went home

and moped around for a week or more, until my mother threatened to start calling people and arranging interviews herself. So I went to grad school — the procrastinator's solution. But anyway," he said, obviously searching for his point. "Oh, well, so, but getting your heart broken is OK, is what I'm trying to tell you boys. Makes you stronger."

"Anybody who breaks their hearts," Mom vowed, "I'll scratch her eyes out."

I tried to hold in a smile for that. *Go get 'em, Mom. Jump the fence and break down Zoe's door.*

Dad shook his head. "Sweetie, I'm making a point. I just want to tell you something, boys, to store away for when you're older, now that you're moving into auditioning, trying for objectives that are difficult for you." He said all this to Jonas, and only then seemed to remember there were two of us sitting on the bench there. "And even the asking-out-girls arena," he added in a generous sort of voice, like, *Well, son, don't worry. Not everybody can sing.*

Jonas sighed, beside me, and whispered, "Sorry."

"The fact is," Dad orated, "sometimes you'll get your hearts broken, and there's nothing even your mother can do to stop that from happening, or me, regardless of how desperately we'd like to protect you both from ever being hurt. You have to get hurt, right, boys?"

"Right, Dad," I said in my most macho voice. "Ugh. Makes us stronger."

He glared at me.

I stood up. "Can we bowl now? We get it."

"One more thing, wise guy, something I would like you to listen to."

I flopped back down.

"You, particularly, play it cool. But there is something to be said for falling in love — with an idea or a woman or an endeavor —"

I dumped my head into my palms. *SHUT UP!* What could be more disgusting than having your father say stuff like *woman* at you?

But on he went. "Even if you do eventually get your heart stomped. Your brother put himself out there, auditioning for this group, and you could learn something from him, Tommy, if you'd let yourself."

I banged the backs of my bowling shoes against the shiny floor and didn't lift my head.

"There's something miraculous about the feeling of knowing what you want and then going for it. Am I right, Jonas?"

I didn't hear a noise from Jonas. Point for him.

"Of experiencing a depth of feeling you rarely get a taste of in life, the feeling that makes your legs tremble and your mouth go dry, but at the same time energizes you, makes you feel more alive than ever before or again — that feeling is actually even more powerful than the slap in the face or the rejection letter that might follow."

I was closer to vomiting than a person not on the bathroom floor should ever be.

"Did Mom slap you in the face when you asked her out?" Jonas asked him. I felt myself smirking, but kept my head bent.

"Not very hard," Mom answered.

Dad stood up and whispered, "Pretty hard," to me and Jonas.

"And only the first time he asked," Mom added.

Dad walked up toward the ball return, but stopped beside Mom. "It was worth it," he said, bending down to kiss her on the hair.

sixteen

The heat wave broke. The next morning, Saturday morning, I woke up at 5:45, when it was still dark. I listened hard for a few minutes, thinking some noise must've woken me up — Jonas calling, the shower water running — but there was nothing, just quiet.

I threw off the covers and sat up, my legs dangling off the bed. My calves ached a little, which let me know I'd probably grown some overnight. I dropped to the floor and did twenty-five push-ups and fifty sit-ups, then lay back on my rug for a while, sweating just a bit but for good reason. I'd so much rather sweat from exercise than humiliation.

I flipped over onto my stomach and did twenty-five

more push-ups, to try to drive the memory of yesterday out of my head. It didn't work. I couldn't figure out how to think about it, what went wrong, why she didn't like me. I decided to just forget the whole thing. No big deal. I hit the bathroom then sneaked downstairs, avoiding steps two and four, to help myself to a massive bowl of cereal and a seat in front of the TV, to zone out for a good long time.

When everybody else got up and started talking, asking questions, chatting, I went back upstairs. I was just going to throw on some clothes and head outside, but at the last second I decided to take a shower. I'm old enough now, whether Dad knows it or not, that it's starting to matter to me if people see me outside with bed-head.

Nobody seemed to have woken up in Zoe's room, I noticed when I happened to glance out the bathroom window. Her shade was still down when I got out of the shower, and when I finished drying off, too.

I used gel in my hair. Mom thinks it looks very attractive that way, and it's no big deal to do it, just takes a second.

I grabbed my tennis racquet and a fresh can of balls. I like the sound it makes when you pop the metal top off. *Chi-koo.* I dropped it on my desk and noticed my key. On its string, on my desk. Weird. I picked it up and held it for a minute, then searched my desk for the penny that had gotten lost. Just in case. Maybe my luck was turning around, I couldn't help thinking, but when I didn't find a penny there, I shook my head at my own silliness. I don't believe in that stuff at all. I'm just kidding around. Of course.

I found my high-tops down in the mud room and stomped them on, then banged out to the driveway and started hitting balls. I hit them as loud as I could. It's good practice, hitting hard and chasing them down.

If she hears me and comes out, I thought, *that's fine.* It's a free country. She can hit tennis balls with me, I don't care. I didn't look over at her back door. Well, hardly at all.

All summer, any time I came out and hit balls against the garage, she came out and joined me. It was like a thing, a signal; we never said anything to each other, and I would never have thought of calling her up and asking if she wanted to hit with me or anything. Just, one of us would go out and start hitting and the other one would hear and come out, even if you were in the middle of a TV show or a conversation or anything, it was like an unspoken rule, you'd have to go out and hit. One time I must've not heard her out there, because she came over and rang the doorbell to get me, and asked if I wanted to hit. I was in the middle of a Monopoly game with Jonas and I owned Park Place with a hotel on it, but I blew it off because it was just what we did. Jonas got all smirky about it, but I went out and hit with her anyway. I only felt bad I'd made her come to the door; I should've just been out there with her.

So officially I could go ring her doorbell.

It would be better if she didn't come out, of course. I'd rather not have to deal with her, after yesterday, anyway, and there's nothing left to say so what would be the point?

I hit for over an hour. It wasn't a hot day, but I was pretty sweaty by the time I finally called it quits. She never did come out. Just as well. I didn't really want her to, that much, anyway.

Not if she didn't want to.

Rachel Vail has written many well-received novels for adolescents, including *Wonder*, an *American Bookseller* "Pick of the Lists," which Judy Blume called "Wonderful!"; *Daring to Be Abigail*, a *School Library Journal* Best Book of the Year; *Do-Over*, a Recommended Book for Reluctant Young Readers; and *Ever After*, which was one of the New York Public Library's 100 Best Children's Books in 1994. She lives with her husband and two sons in New York City.